What the Critics are saying...

Dragon's Kiss

"...Tielle has graduated to the fantasy genre with flying colors. I do look forward to read her next installments in what promises to be an extraordinarily EROTIC ride. With that being said, make sure that you have the a/c cranked up all the way to high, and iced tea or icy cold water readily available to pour -- NOT DRINK -- over your head..." – *Mireya Orsini, Sensual Romance*

"An utterly remarkable tale. Dragon's Kiss by Tielle St. Clare is a scorcher, replete with palpable sexual tension, sensuality and unbelievably steamy sex scenes." – *Sharyn McGinty, In The Library Reviews*

Simon's Bliss

"Ms. St. Claire creates a wonderful balance of tension, sensuality, and uncertainty in her characters for an enjoyable read... I highly recommend this thrilling page-turner." – *Maryellen Kunkel, Sensual Romance*

Irish Enchantment

"*Irish Enchantment* is a well-conceived group of stories. The prologue and characters create a continuity that is maintained throughout all three stories. Each individual story stands alone and offers readers a unique variation on finding love. When all three stories are combined, you can't go wrong." – *Amanda, Fallen Angel Reviews*

DRAGON'S KISS
An Ellora's Cave Publication, October 2004

Ellora's Cave Publishing, Inc.
PO Box 787
Hudson, OH 44236-0787

ISBN #1419950371

ISBN MS Reader (LIT) ISBN # 1-84360-520-1
Other available formats (no ISBNs are assigned):
Adobe (PDF), Rocketbook (RB), Mobipocket (PRC) & HTML

Edited by Ann Richardson
Cover art by Syneca

Warning:

The following material contains graphic sexual content meant for mature readers. *Dragon's Kiss* has been rated E-rotic by a minimum of three independent reviewers.

Ellora's Cave Publishing offers three levels of Romantica™ reading entertainment: S (S-ensuous), E (E-rotic), and X (X-treme).

S-*ensuous* love scenes are explicit and leave nothing to the imagination.

E-*rotic* love scenes are explicit, leave nothing to the imagination, and are high in volume per the overall word count. In addition, some E-rated titles might contain fantasy material that some readers find objectionable, such as bondage, submission, same sex encounters, forced seductions, etc. E-rated titles are the most graphic titles we carry; it is common, for instance, for an author to use words such as "fucking", "cock", "pussy", etc., within their work of literature.

X-*treme* titles differ from E-rated titles only in plot premise and storyline execution. Unlike E-rated titles, stories designated with the letter X tend to contain controversial subject matter not for the faint of heart.

Dragon's Kiss

By Tielle St. Clare

Chapter 1

The fire burned across her skin, searing its memory into her flesh. Forever would she feel its touch. Crave it. The heat entered her body as a roaring flame and melted the frozen depths of her heart. Need filled her—turning her fear into desire.

She twisted on the bed, trying to tear free of the dream. She knew it was a dream, knew it was only her mind holding her captive but she had no power. She couldn't break its grip.

Mine.

The voice whispered through her soul and she shook her head.

No!

Her dream-self raced through the forest, running from the creature that wanted to claim her, consume her. He was behind her, ever nearer.

"No, no, please."

Fire broke out across the sky and surrounded her, trapping her. She stopped, faced with the wall of flames. Spinning around, she faced him.

Black eyes stared at her. Inhuman eyes that warned of lust and death. Flames dribbled from his mouth, licking at her legs. She felt the heat but it didn't burn. His long neck craned forward, moving his massive head toward her body. She stumbled backward and fell to the ground. The rough wool gown flipped up, baring her legs to her thighs. She tried to pull the material down but the creature was there. He nuzzled her hand aside and moved forward, pressing the blunt end of his nose against her sex.

The beast's voice filled her head.
Mine.

"No!"

Lorran's scream shattered the dream. She jerked awake as her own voice reverberated through the cabin. The rapid patter of her heart filled her ears, blocking out all sound. She rolled over, curling onto her side and staring blankly across the room.

She could feel him. He was near, ready to possess her. She shivered despite the warmth of her blankets. The creature hadn't wanted to capture her—he'd wanted to possess her, own her very soul.

Dreams had haunted her for years—horrifying images of flames and death. The screams of the victims. But never like this. Never before had she felt her own vulnerability.

She stared into the pale morning light, unwilling to release the scant comfort of her bed and the childish need to hide under the blankets. The dream was still with her.

The scuffle of heavy feet followed by a loud thump on her front door dragged her from under the bedcovers. She pulled on a robe but hesitated at the door. The villagers hadn't exactly welcomed her. There was no reason anyone would visit her at this hour, or any hour for that matter. Except to demand that she leave. Again.

After the terrifying dream, she wasn't up to more threats.

She waited.

The pounding repeated.

"Mistress! We've need of your help." The deep voice was unfamiliar. "Mistress, are you there?"

It didn't sound like a threat. Still cautious, she cracked open the door and peeked out.

Nothing could have prepared her for the sight. A huge man dressed in full battle leathers with a broad sword belted to his hip crowded her as she opened the door.

"Yes?" she said, backing away as he pressed forward. He entered her house and she saw the reason for his haste—a man, equally as large, draped over his right shoulder. Blood stained the scarred battle leathers covering his legs and the white linen shirt he wore.

"Where can I put him?"

"There," she said, pointing to the bed in the corner. The tiny cabin didn't allow for more than one room. She slept, ate and lived in the single space. Now she'd just offered her bed to a wounded man.

The stranger stalked to the small bed. In a quick but gentle move, he shrugged his burden off his shoulder and caught him, lowering the body onto the mattress. As he stepped away, Lorran saw the truth—the man wasn't just wounded.

A large gouge opened his chest. Blood drenched the torn shirt and dripped down the man's face. She looked at the chest wound.

"That's a dragon bite," she said, speaking the obvious.

"Yes. I couldn't risk taking him to town. I heard you had an interest in dragons."

She nodded. That was probably the nicest thing anyone in town had said about her. Usually they called her a dragon whore.

"Can you help him?"

He asked the question simply. But the answer wasn't simple.

Lorran looked into his eyes. He was young but the grim light of determination told her he knew the wounded man's fate.

"I can nurse him. It will depend on the Gods if he survives."

"And if he survives?" He stared at her with a warrior's eyes — cold and deadly. "Can you help him?"

She knew what he was asking. The warrior waited. She thought about lying, considered giving him the answer he wanted to hear, what anyone would want to hear at this point.

But she couldn't.

"I don't know." She looked down at the torn and crumpled body. The faint smell of sulfur clung to his clothes. Dragonfire. Burn marks stained his leather trousers and the edges of his shirt. The leather chest protector that should have been there was gone. "I can try," she finally said.

"Is there hope? Is there some possibility that it can be stopped?" He placed his hand on the hilt of the broad sword that hung at his waist. "I need to know."

Emotions welled up in Lorran's chest at the subtle threat. She knew what would happen if she said no. The man would die. Better to die than...

"Yes." She turned away. She didn't lie well and feared it might show in her face. She looked at the wounded man. There was something familiar about him. "The sooner I tend to him, the better chance he has." That was a lie as well, but at least it would give her something to do. And it was something to distract the soldier who waited for an answer. She glanced up as she moved to collect water and cloth to clean the wound. The soldier didn't believe her — it was obvious on his face — but maybe, he wanted some hope to cling to as well. In the end, it wouldn't matter. The truth would reveal itself soon enough.

"Do what you can." With that command, he turned and stalked to the door.

"Wait! Where are you going?" She hurried behind him. He couldn't just leave a wounded stranger in her care — particularly not one suffering from a dragon bite. Dragon bites were too uncertain. And the potential damage was too great.

"I have to return," he said, stepping onto the porch. "If rumor gets out that he's been attacked, we'll have a rebellion on our hands."

Lorran watched him walk away. "But — but — I don't know how to get a hold of you. How do you want me to contact you?"

"I'll send a guard from the Castle daily for updates as to his progress."

"The Castle? Who are you?" She looked at the bloodied man in her bed. "Who is he?"

"I'm Riker. That's Kei."

Lorran felt the blood drain from her face.

"Kei the Dragon Slayer," she said unnecessarily.

"Yes." Riker turned and walked away, climbing on the back of his horse before calling out his final instruction. "Tell no one who he is or that he's here. The safety of the kingdom could depend on it."

His long hair caught the breeze as he kicked the flanks of his horse, spurring the beast along. Lorran watched until he was out of sight and she was left alone to tend to the man who'd killed her husband.

✳ ✳ ✳ ✳ ✳

Fire burned through his chest. The flame entered his blood and rode the veins through the depths of his body, burning away the traces of humanity and leaving behind a new creature. The man's body burned. He arched up, pressing down on his shoulders and the heels of his feet, fighting the invasion but it was too late. The beast was there, invading the empty corners of his soul.

"Shh. Relax. Breathe for me. Breathe." The voice poured over his body like cool water, smothering the fire. The tension faded and he dropped back onto the bed. "That's it. Breathe. Long, deep breaths." His eyes were glued shut by pain but he tried to follow her orders. He inhaled and filled his lungs with her scent. It reminded him of sun-warmed hay and a fresh pine wood fire. The sweet smell eased him even further. "That's it. Sleep."

Even with his eyes closed, he could feel her moving away. His hand shot out, snagging her thin wrist. The tiny bone would crack in his hand if he wished it. He tried to ease his grip but couldn't force his hand to relax.

"Stay." The voice didn't sound like his but he knew it was. The memories were returning. He had no idea how long he'd been here or how long he'd been caught in the fire. "Please," he added, some latent etiquette emerging.

"Of course. I'll stay."

She was lying. He knew it. She'd stay until he was asleep and then she'd run. Instinct screamed at him to grab her, hold her. Bind her to him so she couldn't escape.

The human in him grew sick at the thought.

Kei willed his fingers to uncurl from around her wrist. His soul wailed in pain but he rolled away, turning his back to the woman.

He curled his arm beneath his head and concentrated, feeling his body from the inside out. Something was strange—invading his senses, becoming a part of him.

He couldn't open his eyes but he knew Riker was gone. Left alone with the female. He breathed in again and recognized her scent, tasted it on his lips. She was strange, yet familiar. Fog crept over his mind, easing him into sleep—a sleep clouded with dreams.

The woman was there. He couldn't see her face but he knew her taste. Intimately knew her taste. She lay spread before him, offering herself to him. Knowing he was welcome, that she sought his touch, he sank down before her and placed his mouth against her wet, hot sex open to him.

It was perfect. This was what he'd craved all his life. Her flavor, her scent, the feel of her skin against his. He had to have her, hold her.

Panic like he'd never felt in all his years as a warrior dug into his gut, wrapping itself around his genitals like an iron fist. She would leave him. He couldn't let her leave him.

She faded from his hands, disappearing and reappearing a few feet away. He crawled toward her—she backed away. He reached for her. Fear flared in her eyes. She turned, dodging his grip. He clutched at her fading figure. He had to have her, had to keep her. She vanished.

No. Mine! The word raged in his head. She was gone. The heart-crushing panic was on him again and he fought it, sought the strength of a warrior, the stoic face he'd learned as a child. All that remained was silence.

She was gone.

She'd left him.

* * * * *

Lorran chewed on her thumbnail and paced the tiny room. She glanced back every few seconds to the man twisting on her bed. Sweat clung to his body as he struggled. The internal battle would continue. Three days was standard for the trance that accompanied a dragon bite.

He was free of fever. She'd studied enough attacks to know that dragon bites healed quickly and cleanly. But that didn't stop the pain or the torture in the days following the attack. Nothing would ease him.

She'd tried with her husband but her presence had served only to enrage him.

Still, compassion welled up inside her. She couldn't stand to see another human suffer. Giving in to the emotion, she turned her steps across the room and sank down on the edge of the bed.

"Your Majesty, please." He twisted on the sheets fighting and tearing. "Please, Your Majesty." *Dammit*, she said to her herself. Calling him "Your Majesty" was going to get old. Quickly. She took a deep breath. "Kei, everything will be all right." She didn't know what else to say. Even though lying was against her nature. She wanted to comfort him. "It will be fine," she repeated. Her voice seemed to reach him and he stilled. He never opened his eyes but he turned in her direction. "That's it. Everything will be fine. I promise."

She placed her hand on his shoulder. The warm muscle jumped beneath her fingertips. She'd pulled the tattered shirt from his chest while she'd cleaned the wound. She'd left his battle leathers on while she'd bandaged the torn flesh. But bandages were almost worthless on a dragon bite. The wound was already beginning to heal.

Kei sighed as she continued to lightly rub her palm across his shoulder. She watched the tension ease from his body. Sleep was the best thing for him. Lorran sat for a moment. She'd stay with him until he settled.

It had been five years since she'd seen him — and then it had been after a brief and bloody fight. She wouldn't have recognized him if she'd seen him in the street. His face had matured, losing any soft edges of youth and gaining none of the roundness from excess. His long blond hair was spread across her pillow, framing his masculine face.

He looked every inch a king. Even with his wild hair and bare chest, he looked powerful. Having moved to this kingdom after her husband's death, she was unfamiliar with the royal family. She wasn't a part of that world any longer. If she remembered correctly, he'd been raised as a warrior, never expecting to be crowned king. She knew why he'd been chosen to lead. This was a man born to rule — a warrior leading a kingdom of warriors.

Women had been rumored to swoon when he looked at them, so handsome was his face. The sharp cut of his cheekbones and a pale scar next to his eye saved him from any kinship to feminine beauty. His face was carved stone, hard even in rest. She couldn't see the color of his eyes but reports said they were crystal-clear green, the color of new grass.

And soon, all this human beauty would be gone.

Emotions flip-flopped through her mind. Anger at finally facing the man who'd killed Brennek, but compassion as well. How strange was fate that his justice had been delivered in such a fashion? She felt no triumph. No human should have to live through the next three weeks of this man's life.

The silence of the cabin grew oppressive as she sat beside him. Her thoughts began to rattle with things she had to accomplish before daylight ended. There was still work to be done. How long would it take for him to fall asleep? She had things to do—notes to make. It wasn't often that anyone got the chance to study a dragon's victim from bite until the conclusion. She needed to write down her observations.

She looked down at him. His eyes were closed but not squeezed shut in pain, his shoulders seemed relaxed, his breathing even. He was finally resting.

She leaned forward, preparing to stand. His hand slipped across the blankets and landed softly on her leg, holding her. The grip was firm but not painful. Lorran froze. He was asleep. It had to be some kind of reflex. His tan skin looked pale against the dark wool of her skirt. White lines criss-crossed the back of his hand telling of his warrior's life. He may be a king now, but he had been raised a soldier.

Lorran reached down to remove his hand but instead he moved, slipping his large palm up her leg, curling it to match the curve of her thigh, delving his fingers into the space between her legs.

Lorran looked around the empty room, as if someone might see her with a man's hand on her thigh. It was an intimate touch but it couldn't be intentional. The man was asleep or, at minimum, in a healing trance. He obviously didn't know what he was doing.

Kei had a certain reputation but Lorran doubted even *he* could attempt a seduction just hours after being bitten by a dragon.

His fingers pushed downward, then up, until they brushed the juncture of her thighs.

"Or maybe he could," she said aloud. The flutter of his fingers against her sex stopped her words. This couldn't be happening. It had been years, *years* since any hand but hers had touched there. Now a stranger, and a king no less, was doing so.

She squirmed, trying to subtly remove him. Instead, Kei's fingers insinuated themselves deeper between her legs until he cupped her, forming his fingers to the line of her sex. A fluttered pleasure zipped through her stomach.

"Please, Your Majesty, Kei...your hand..." She tugged on the heavy weight of his wrist. He growled softly and the lines across his forehead deepened. "Kei, I don't think—" He pressed one long finger along her pussy, teasing her clit with a light touch. "Oh, my." She tensed, sitting up straight on the bed. "I really think—oh dear..." With slow easy strokes, he began massaging her. A spike of need shot through her center. She inhaled sharply. *How can this be happening? The man is asleep!* His fingers continued to move, the rhythm changing to steady pulses. He seemed to know just where to touch her, the perfect intensity.

"This is a bad idea. I shouldn't let him do this," she told the empty room. But her body ignored the logic of her words. She leaned back and arched her hips upward, opening her legs until he had full access. A soft rumble sounded from Kei's throat—a contented, pleased noise, like the purr of a satisfied lion. He rubbed his whole hand up and down, fully massaging her sensitive lips, increasing the tension across her clit. The light wool of her skirt only heightened the sensation. The heat of his touch flowed through the material and warmed her skin.

Her sex was wet and empty. She moaned softly at the sudden sharp desire to be filled.

Lorran pressed the tips of her fingers into the solid wall of his chest. Her hips rolled in gentle movements as she searched for more of the sensations his hand pulled from deep inside her body. She arched against his fingers, pushing him against her clit, focusing his touch and guiding him.

Heat poured from his fingers and flowed through her pussy, driving her on. The pressure grew. Her shallow breath bounced off the cabin walls, echoing back and filling her ears with the sound. Her hips pumped with certainty now, the sweet tightening building until in one sharp moment, it evaporated, released, scattering tendrils of heat through her body. Lorran tensed and held herself still. The wild pleasure captured her, then slowly faded through her body.

After long moments, when her breath returned to normal, she looked down. She'd left tiny nail marks on Kei's chest.

He didn't seem to notice. He slept, his hand still between her legs, but calmed, not moving. The hint of a smile hovered over his lips—as if he knew what he'd done.

"If that's what he can do in his sleep, no wonder women swoon before him," she whispered.

She continued to sit beside him, half-amazed at what she'd let happen and half-stunned that Kei seemed to have slept through it all. Finally, his breathing evened out and she realized he was truly asleep. When she stood, he let her go with no more than a mumbled protest.

Her freedom lasted twenty minutes before he began to twist on the bed and tear at the bedclothes. She returned to his side and placed her fingers lightly against his chest. He immediately quieted and his hand inched toward her thigh.

"Oh, it's going to be an interesting couple of days."

The next two days were nothing short of exhausting. And confusing. She couldn't step away from Kei for more than a few minutes without him reacting—struggling against an invisible force. Her presence seemed to allow him to rest and eased the fury. She spent the days sitting beside him, always touching. The contact seemed vital to keep him calm.

It was no hardship for Lorran. He had a beautiful body. The warm muscles fit perfectly beneath her hands. She tried to keep the touch impersonal but sometimes she just had to smooth her palms across the strong plane of his chest or the powerful leg muscles. Kei seemed to enjoy this the most—sighing and moaning, growling when she stopped.

But all of that would have been endurable. It was the power he seemed to have over her body that drained all her energy. His hand continually sought out and found the hot space between her legs. It was only after he'd brought her to orgasm that he'd fall into a real sleep. She lost track of how many times she'd found herself moaning and pleading with him to let her come.

The nights were the hardest. Initially, she'd tried setting up a small cot but he'd moaned and twisted until she'd crawled onto the bed with him. He'd instantly calmed, snuggling against her, despite the distance she tried to put between their bodies.

Each night, he'd wrap himself around her, his strong arms holding her back to his front, curling into her until she felt surrounded. Then his hand would move unerringly towards the vee of her thighs. And it would begin again. Her gown blocked direct contact but the weight of his hand and the light flutter of his fingers sent layers of shivers through her body.

Removing his hand was not an option. She tried that. Like a child with its favorite toy taken away, he grumbled and groaned. The struggle became a nightly event where Lorran would eventually give up and allow his hand to remain.

In response, Kei sighed, smiled and cuddled against her, content to have his way.

And then he'd begin the tiny movements, subtle touches that became caresses, finally bringing her to climax—sometimes hard and fast, sometimes long and deep. It didn't matter. Each night, Lorran found herself, her legs opened, pressing against his strong fingers, anxious for the release his touch promised.

Once she'd climaxed, Kei would pull her to him, turning her onto her back and settling his head on her breasts. The slight smile that marked his lips told her that somewhere, deep inside the sleeping man, *someone* knew what he was doing.

Hours passed before Lorran allowed herself to drop into a light doze.

The dawn of the third day pulled Lorran out of the bed. She instantly missed the warmth of Kei's body. Kei grumbled in protest but let her go. Moving quickly, she stoked the fire and began her morning routine, enjoying the quiet. She got breakfast and tidied the small cabin, finishing up at Kei's side.

It would be over soon. Sometime in the next twenty-four hours, Kei would open his eyes and stare at her in confusion. And possibly revulsion. She doubted he would remember the intimate touches he'd given her. And she'd never tell.

She stared down at his bare form, the sheet gone in a flurry of twists and turns. He was magnificently made. The broad line of his chest rippled with full tight muscles. His arms, even in rest, showed their power. She followed the taut line of his stomach. His cock was half-hard. He'd spent the last three days in that state. He shifted restlessly on the bed and Lorran raised her gaze.

How long would it be before the beast showed itself? She stared at his body, trying to distance herself, trying to separate the woman from the observer. Had the changes already begun? The memory of her husband's transition was a blur, vague images filled with pain and disappointment. She hadn't been there when he'd made the final change. She'd never learned what caused it, only seen the destruction later.

She trailed her fingers across Kei's chest. She'd grown used to touching him in the past two days. He instantly calmed, his body relaxing at her light touch.

This was such an opportunity. She could observe him—watch him. So much could be done if they could learn how the transition was accomplished. More and more information about dragons was becoming available—but the chance to monitor a full transition was rare.

She watched Kei all day. Slowly, the healing trance faded and he fell into a true sleep. It was over. Lorran walked away and he didn't protest. She stayed away as she cooked dinner and prepared for bed. He didn't seem to notice.

Kei no longer needed her. The odd ache of disappointment that lingered in her chest made her cringe. She was upset that a sick man and a crazed beast no longer needed her presence. *How pathetic.*

When it was time for bed, she sank down on the small cot. Kei had been sleeping peacefully. She pulled the blanket up over her warm nightgown and watched him in the dark. It was strange but she'd already grown used to feeling his weight on her body as she slept. She blew out the final candle and closed her eyes.

Kei's moans woke her a short time later. He twisted on the bed, a contained version of the struggles from the early part of the trance. She slipped out of the blankets and sat on the edge of his bed. He was cool to the touch and once again calmed when she placed her hand on his skin. It was late. One final night. She slid under the bedclothes next to him and settled down. Morning would come soon enough.

Kei immediately wrapped his arms around her and sighed contentedly. Lorran had to crush a similar sound from escaping her lips. She closed her eyes and was asleep almost instantly.

He was there, stalking her through the dark forest, waiting for her as she stepped into the dream world.
Mine.

The voice was back, commanding her attention.

The dragon's head swung toward her. His huge mouth opened and fire burst from the depths of his throat, covering her, consuming her. The flames surrounded her, licking at her skin like a million fiery tongues.

She waited for the pain but there was none, only the flurry of fire against her flesh, the rush of warmth inside.

She welcomed the heat that slid across her skin, concentrating in the deep, moist center of her body. Tiny licks of flame moved down her neck. Instinct guided her reaction. She tilted her head and let the warmth touch her skin — hot but not burning, not wounding.

Heat invaded her lungs and tightened her chest. A molten band circled her waist, pulling her deep into the fire. She needed it inside her.

She didn't know what was happening to her. An invisible force surrounded her body like a fever. She tried to open her eyes, needing to see the beast who held her captive, but she couldn't make her eyes respond to her commands.

She opened her mouth to plead with it and she was consumed. Streaks of liquid heat flowed over her skin, inflaming her breasts. She spread her legs and let the flame touch her. It burned against her. Then the fire was inside her, igniting the core of her body. The tendrils flicked in an uneven rhythm, slipping inside, then teasing her protective lips. She pressed her hips upward. The fever burned conscious thought from her mind. Her only understanding was the need to accept the flame into her body.

Mine.

The angry powerful pronouncement should have terrified her. Somewhere deep in her soul, she was frightened but the fear was crushed by the intensity of the fire. She wanted to drown in the warmth.

Fingers of heat danced across her sex, skimming the dark curled hair and tickling the flesh beneath it. She arched her hips, seeking more of his touch. He was there, a stranger yet so familiar. Her legs opened wider, inviting him inside.

The material of her gown stretched tight as she struggled to get closer to the heat. Hands appeared to help her. The edges of her bodice separated. She felt a cool brush of air before the fire claimed her breasts. Hot hands cupped her, rasping her taut nipples that poked out, begging for his touch. She arched up, seeking more of the incredible sensation. The voice rumbled with triumph and a warm mouth closed over the tip of her breast. He suckled her, drawing her flesh into his mouth and teasing it with his tongue.

The ache between her thighs built. Then, the large warm hand returned to her sex, cupping her moist center and driving two fingers deep inside.

She pumped her hips — counter to the steady thrust of his fingers, wanting him deeper.

"Mine!"

The voice was real and jolted Lorran from her dream. Awareness pierced the surreal fog.

Kei's mouth covered her breast and his hand was hard between her bare legs, thrusting slow steady strokes in and out of her sex.

She yelped. Her mind commanded instant action and she threw herself from the bed, ripping her body from Kei's grasp and rolling to the floor. She gathered the edges of her torn nightgown together. Kei's eyes flicked downward. She reached down to ensure her gown covered her legs.

Kei propped his head up on his hand. The arrogant smile held none of the desperate need that his feverish rantings had displayed. This was a man, confident in his attraction, sure of his welcome.

There was no evidence of the dragon bite he'd suffered only three days before. After long moments of inspection, he lifted his gaze to hers and smiled.

"No need to run, darling. We're just getting started."

Chapter 2

Kei looked across the tiny space at the woman. She pulled the sides of her torn gown together, trying to cover the soft, sweet mounds of flesh beneath. Startled passion began to fade in her eyes.

Who is she?

He tried to remember how he got here but all that occupied his mind was a black haze filled with screams and fire. And heat. Wet, female heat.

His eyes dropped to the thin layer of cloth that hid her pussy from his gaze. She was wet. His hand still held the evidence.

More.

He drew in a deep breath and was assaulted by the sweet scent of her arousal. He had to have her. Had to taste her. A strange dark fog brushed the edges of his mind, blurring his thoughts and filling him with a desperate need for this woman. Moving as if driven by a force outside himself, Kei crawled from the bed and started towards the woman. The craving to gorge himself on her boiled inside him.

A voice in the distant corner of his mind whispered that he should stop—she might be frightened—but it was drowned out by the need to place his mouth on her sex, drink from her cunt. Drive his tongue deep inside her.

The woman watched him and inched backward on her hands until she ran into the wall.

"Mine," he whispered as he got near. The overwhelming sense of ownership stopped him for a moment, but then she shifted and more of her sweet smell came to him.

The pull to have her was too strong to listen to the quiet call for restraint. His hands gripped the bottom of her light gown, ready to tear the garment away. Then he looked in her eyes.

Amazement alternated with fear in the brown depths. The strange voice in his head pushed him onward, drawing him to her. He needed to fill himself with her flavor.

She licked her lips and swallowed deeply. He held her gaze as he slid the gown up her legs, revealing her naked pussy. The delicious scent flowed over him. She was wet and waiting for him.

The sound of her labored breathing teased him. He was tempted to drop his gaze to her luscious breasts, but he didn't want to break the spell of her eyes. She was his. She belonged to him.

The soft material of her nightgown flowed over his arms as he slipped his hands underneath. Her bare flesh burned him and he knew—this was the fire he craved. This fire would warm him forever.

His cock was hard, eager to plunge inside her wet cunt but he waited. The need to fill his senses with her pushed hard against him. It was imperative that he consume all that was her.

He slipped his hands up her legs, cupping her ass in his palms and pulled her toward him, cocking her hips forward. She gasped but she didn't protest. The soft mounds of her backside filled his hands nicely and he momentarily considered future opportunities for that ass.

He lowered his gaze. She was almost on her back, her legs spread wide, her sweet pussy open to him.

Mine.

He fell forward and covered her sex with his mouth. For a moment, he simply tasted her, drowning in the seductive flavor that lured him to her. He licked her slit, drinking the moisture her body offered up to him. Her sharp flavor seduced his tongue and he sipped again.

Yes. More.

The drive was almost more than he could endure. He slipped his tongue inside her cunt. And the world slowed. This was where he needed to be. He flicked his tongue along the inside edge of her pussy. Then plunged deep, as far as he could reach. She gasped and pushed against him.

Kei stilled her movements, holding her in place for his pleasure—and for hers. *Mine.*

Lorran dug her hands into his hair, using the long strands as her anchor to this world. Goddesses, what was he doing to her? This was beyond anything. His tongue fluttered around her sex, lingering moments on her clit before trailing a long path across her wet, open flesh. Then he dipped his strong tongue inside and flicked the end, tickling the walls of her passage. His soft, approving growls were muffled against her flesh.

"Aah!" Her head thumped against the wall behind her.

The heat had returned but now instead of a vague creature made of fire, the source was Kei the Dragon Slayer. Somewhere in a quiet corner of her mind, she knew she should stop him. But the fire gathered inside her and she couldn't break free. She needed the heat to survive.

The thought was there and gone in a moment, scattered by the slow glide of his tongue the length of her sex. He stopped, holding on the sensitive nub that screamed for his attention. He opened his mouth and began to suck.

The guttural cry that broke from her lips seemed to come from another creature but Lorran couldn't control it.

She sat up, dislodging Kei from his place. With a gentle snarl, he placed a hand on her stomach pushed her back against the wall and continued to suckle.

"Kei—I mean, Your Majesty, oh Hells, please. Majesty…Kei!" His nightly fondling had trained her body, taught her to expect release, but never this wild, unrelenting pleasure—pain. It had to stop but she couldn't find a way to pull back.

She pressed her fingers into his scalp. "Please, Kei, help me."

She didn't think he heard. Then the pressure of his tongue changed into steady, rhythmic pulses against her clit. She felt her eyes widen as the world spiraled down to one central point between her thighs. She ground her pussy into his face—trying to bring him deeper. He purred and kept sucking. He reached up, slipping two long fingers inside her cunt. The pressure was incredible. Lorran gasped as the fire that had invaded her dreams shattered and spilled across her body.

She blinked rapidly and stared blankly at the empty room.

Her heart thudded in her chest, her breath trying to catch up to the furious beat. Satisfaction dragged her eyelids down. She sagged against the wall and listened to the sound of Kei's contented sighs.

His tongue circled her belly button. She groaned. A spike of renewed warmth pierced her stomach. It was beginning again. How was it that this man had such control over her body?

She opened her eyes and watched the warrior lying between her legs. He was totally absorbed as he continued to taste her flesh, as if he couldn't get enough of her. She could feel the hard press of his erection against her leg. Would he mount her? Would she let him? He had to desire release soon, but instead of moving up, he resettled his face between her thighs.

And spread her sex wide with his fingers.

"Kei—" Whatever she'd been ready to say died as he placed his mouth over her cunt and slipped the firm point of his tongue inside, licking the walls. Her body, sensitized by his touch, trembled and creamed at this light, teasing caress. He was unrelenting, lightly flicking his tongue along the edges of her sex, his movements casual as if he had no goal. He just wanted to taste her.

Pounding penetrated Lorran's lust-blurred mind. She sat up. Kei grunted, as if irritated at being dislodged but kept licking. Lorran took a deep breath and tried to focus. Knocking. Someone was at the door. Morning sunlight sprinkled through the tiny kitchen window. The guard from the Castle. He'd be wanting the daily missive Riker had requested.

The knocking sounded again, louder, more aggressive. Kei heard it as well. He jumped to his feet, hunched low, his knees bent, ready for attack. She watched his eyes scan the room. All traces of sensuality evaporated in that moment—he was a warrior, ready to fight the unknown enemy.

Lorran scrambled to standing. "It's just the door," she muttered, hurrying past him. She tugged at the edges of her ripped bodice, trying to cover her breasts. She had no intention of baring her body the Castle guard. She grabbed the note she'd written last night and opened the door, staying safely behind it.

"Good morrow, Mistress," the guard greeted. He was a different man than the other two days. The uniform was more ornate but clearly he was from the Castle. He looked over her shoulder as if trying to see into her cabin.

"Good morrow." She handed him the parchment and started to close the door.

"I've been ordered to see the king myself."

"No," she answered instinctively. There was something about this guard she didn't trust. And the need to protect Kei was strong after three days. Even though he was a king, Kei was at risk now. The sword on the guard's hip could be quickly bared and Kei would be unarmed. "It agitates him if anyone comes near."

She heard another growl echo across the room. "I really can't be away long. Tell them I'll have news tomorrow." She snapped the door shut before the guard could protest.

Then she waited. Kei stood silently behind her. It was time to face him. She took a deep breath and slowly turned around.

His eyes glowed with anger.

"What in the Dark Hells is going on?"

* * * * *

Kei's mind cleared of the strange dark haze that had invaded it as he watched the woman hurry toward the door. *Who is she?* He licked his lips and felt his cock harden even farther. He knew her taste, knew her scent, but he didn't know her name.

A quick check of the cabin told him he wasn't any place familiar.

So he had three questions: where was he, how had he gotten there, and who was the delicious woman who was here to entertain him?

She wasn't his usual style. He tended toward tall, slim women. She was tall enough but her rounded curves were a little beyond his usual preferences. But he had reveled in the taste of her. And wanted more.

She spoke quietly to the person on the doorstep then closed the door with a quick snap. Was she hiding? Or was she hiding him?

Kei folded his arms and waited for her to turn around. She seemed to be hesitating, as if she didn't want to face him.

Who is she? Why did she seem so familiar yet so foreign?

Mine.

The thought lifted his cock. He hadn't fucked her upon waking—too intent on licking her pussy—now, his body felt the deprivation. He wanted her. This was more than a morning erection. He *needed* to put his cock in this woman, to come inside her.

Kei inhaled deeply and willed his thoughts back into his control. He'd been trained as a warrior from childhood. He knew how to live with pain. A little sexual discomfort should be nothing. But that didn't stop his desire.

Finally, the woman straightened her back and slowly turned.

"What in the Dark Hells is going on?" he demanded. He didn't have the time or patience for courtesy. Something was very wrong. Whoever had been at the door had known he was here but she hadn't let him in.

He ignored the fact that he was naked and his cock was so hard he was ready to drive nails into stone and drew himself to his full height. The woman seemed to recognize the change and dropped into a low curtsy.

"Your Majesty," she whispered.

Kei almost smiled. It was ludicrous. He was naked. He'd just been licking her cunt, and now she bowed before him with the elegance of a Peer. He stayed away from women of the Peer Class. They wanted too much. By the Gods, had he somehow gotten drunk and ended up married to the wench? He intended to marry eventually, but he'd hoped to be sober at the event.

She stayed in the low curtsy, her head bowed, waiting for his release.

"Arise," he commanded. She straightened and raised her eyes. Kei was stunned by what he saw there—this was no humble servant. She was staring at him with barely disguised disdain, even some irritation. And maybe a trace of fear.

Hells, what had he done to deserve that?

"May I get you something to wear?" she offered. Her eyes remained locked on his face.

"I'd prefer a few answers first."

"Then may I request that you cover yourself?" She paused as if realizing how demanding she'd sounded. "If it please Your Majesty." She said the right words but they were clearly wrenched from her as an obligation.

"I'm comfortable as I am," he replied, just to be perverse. He widened his stance and propped his hands on his hips so there was no implication that he was hiding. Red tinged her cheeks giving her a delightfully innocent look. She could still blush? Unusual. "Who are you?"

"I'm Lorran, Your Majesty. You're in my cabin, outside of Memph."

Kei took the information and tried to remember arriving. There was nothing. His last memory was entering the dragon's lair. He'd yelled to Riker to be aware and then the world went black—and red. Red filled with pain, blood and burning.

"What's happened? Why am I here?"

The woman took a deep breath and Kei found himself momentarily distracted by the rise and fall of her breasts and the bare skin beneath her gown. He'd torn the front of her nightgown. He'd tasted those nipples, sucked them into his mouth. The need to do so again pushed him, but he clenched his fists and held steady. So, he was attracted to her—that wouldn't stop him from finding out the truth.

"You and your brother went after Effron."

"I remember that."

She took another deep breath as if preparing to give bad news. The hair along his neck stood up.

"Is Riker hurt?" Kei stalked forward and grabbed the woman by her upper arms.

"Oh, no. He's fine," she quickly assured him.

"Well?" He gave her a slight shake, his already stretched patience ready to snap.

She pressed her lips together then nodded. "The dragon attacked. He bit you."

He released her and stepped back. The center of his stomach fell away. "No." He rejected the idea as he had the Demons of the Dark Hells. "No," he repeated.

All his dreams for the kingdom evaporated in the steady gaze from Lorran's brown eyes. She didn't flinch under his fierce stare. *How did this happen?* As soon as the question came to mind, he realized it no longer mattered.

"How long do I have?" The isolation in his voice startled even him.

She glanced away. "It depends. Sometimes it's months."

She was lying and doing a pitifully poor job of it. "How long?" he demanded. He had things to do before his death.

The steel in her spine returned and she looked back at him. "Three weeks. About three weeks."

Kei nodded. He needed clothes. If they were outside of Memph, they were only half a day's hard riding from the Castle.

"Thank you for your care. I assume *you* nursed me back to health?"

She nodded, a vague look of confusion marring her serene face.

"I'll make sure you're compensated, of course." He somehow knew that idea would piss her off. She hadn't helped him out of the hope for money. But why had she? Any other woman would have run screaming from a man bitten by a dragon. The dragon's reputation was well deserved. But he couldn't think about any of that right now. He needed to get home. "Where are my clothes?"

"Destroyed."

He spun around and stared at her. She'd gone too far.

"You destroyed my clothes?!"

"No, the dragon did that. I just took the tattered pieces off your body and burned them." She planted her hands on her hips and the bodice of her gown gaped showing the sweet curve of her full breasts. She'd forgotten the tear he'd made. His palms itched to cup those soft mounds, hold them for his mouth. He licked his lips and stared, amazed at the urge to touch her.

A sweet scent wafted toward him, luring him forward. Now that his mind was clear, it took him a moment to identify it. It was her, her pussy. She was sending him that delicious sun-warmed scent. He licked his lips, the taste of her cunt still on his mouth. An uncomfortable tightening permeated his groin. By the Gods, he was hard, and needed relief. Inside her body. He wanted her. He wanted to fuck her until he was dry and she ached with his pounding.

The stern, disapproving glare in her eyes should have shut down his desires but all Kei could think about was turning her hard eyes soft, making her scream with pleasure, not disapproval. She looked cold, even frigid, but the memory of her response—her wetness as he fingered her, the sweet way she'd moaned as he'd slipped his tongue inside her—told a different story. She wasn't cold. She'd burned him with her fire. He wanted to feel her pussy clinging to his cock as he pushed inside her.

He shook his head to clear it of the image. The urge to take her stayed with him but he gathered the strength that had led him to the throne and focused on what he had to do.

"I need clothes and I need my horse."

"No."

Kei stopped in mid-step across the cabin. Gone were the slightly reluctant tones of respect.

"What?" He was raised as a warrior. Now, crowned a king. People didn't say "no" to him. Not more than once.

"You can't go."

He folded his arms across his chest and kicked his lips up into a half-smile.

"Darling, I appreciate the invitation, but as delectable as you are, I have things to do."

He'd never seen anyone bristle before. She seemed to swell before his eyes and the suppressed look of disdain was freed.

"Your *Majesty*, while I might have endured your pawings while you were in the trance, trust me, it would give me no greater pleasure than to see you walking out my door."

He felt the edge of his lips pull up into a smile. She was a fierce little thing when she got riled.

"Unfortunately, it's a matter of life and death, and while I don't particularly want you here, it's not safe for you to return."

"Why?" he mocked. "Because they'll kill me?" It didn't matter. Death would follow. Better an honorable death than one as—he crushed the thought before it could form.

"No. Because you'll kill them."

* * * * *

Lorran braced herself for his reaction. He was a different creature now that he was free of the trance. Any semblance of vulnerability was gone.

Having cared for his body for three days, she'd known he was large but he towered over her, filling her cabin and making the tiny space seem even smaller. Even the strength she'd observed in his sleep was nothing to the internal power he exuded now. This was a frighteningly strong man—physically and mentally.

And she'd just shocked him. But she had to make him understand. Over the next three weeks, the dragon's awareness would grow inside him, slowly overtaking the human mind. And then, in an instant, the dragon would appear in corporeal form and the human would disappear forever.

"Explain that." It was a true command, spoken by one used to giving orders and expecting them to be filled.

Irritation pricked her. She'd spent three days watching him, soothing him, and allowing him to touch her—though she would admit that had been a pleasure for her—and now he presumed to give her orders like some serf. She was tempted to snap at him but she wanted his help, so she clamped down on the annoyance.

"The change happens more quickly if the man returns home. No one knows why exactly, but it's believed to be the emotional upheaval."

"Emotional upheaval?"

He was obviously a warrior who didn't believe emotions would or could affect him. She took all emotion out of her voice.

"Yes. As the creature begins to awaken, the human is lost more and more. The challenge of trying to maintain the previous personality seems to make the dragon more fierce. More desperate to appear. And more angry when he does appear."

Kei squinted and watched her for a moment. "How do you know so much?" Suspicion laced his voice.

"I study dragons."

And the light of recognition flared in his eyes. "Of course. You're the dragon who—" He stopped and had the grace to look ashamed.

"Don't worry, Your Majesty. I know what they call me."

"And it doesn't bother you?"

Because he sounded truly curious, and not mocking, she answered honestly. "No. Because I have to be near the dragons to study them."

"For what purpose?" The king stared at her in amazement. "The only reason to study them is to find more efficient ways to kill them. The only good dragon is a dead dragon."

Lorran knew most people held that opinion, but still, it was hard to hear the words. She'd come to respect if not understand these creatures.

"I'll be curious to see if you hold that same opinion in three weeks time when you turn into one of those creatures. Will death be your choice?"

"Yes," he answered without pausing. "But I'll never make the final transition. I won't do that to my family or to my people."

Lorran felt her eyes widen. He couldn't be serious. "You'd suicide?" The idea was so foreign she couldn't imagine it. The depth of his determination was beyond her comprehension.

"If that's the only way the transition can be stopped then, yes. You've seen what happens to the villages where these creatures nest. You've seen the destruction, the devastation. Crops burned, entire herds of livestock eliminated. And then, there's the lovely tradition of sacrificing virgins." Kei began to pace the room and for the first time, Lorran saw him as a leader, not merely as a king. He wasn't blind with hatred. He hated with reason. "No matter how many times we tell people that sacrificing virgins doesn't help, they still do it. And the dragon still takes them." He spun around and stalked toward her. "Have you seen what happens to these women when the dragon is done with them?" He stopped in front of her. "Have you?"

"Yes," she whispered, the memories still haunted her dreams. She'd never been able to save them. Their screams of terror had eventually ended in death.

"And still you defend them?"

Lorran didn't know how to respond. "I have my reasons." Reasons a warrior like Kei the Dragon Slayer wouldn't understand.

He cocked his head to the side and stared at her.

"You look familiar." It was a question spoken without asking.

Lorran looked away, choosing not to answer.

"Why do I know you?" he asked more directly.

"How would I know what you know, Your Majesty? May I find you something to wear?" She didn't wait for an answer, simply walked by him, her head held high, her eyes averted from his nakedness. Not that it helped. She knew intimately what the man looked like, felt like. The image of his form was burned into her memory and it would take years if not a lifetime to blur them beyond recognition. But that didn't mean she couldn't *act* like she wasn't aware.

She opened the closet door. A few of Brennek's clothes remained. She'd carried them around instead of getting rid of them despite the fact that they held little sentimental value. Now, she was glad. They would be tight on Kei but at least he'd be clothed and she could begin her campaign to forget his naked body.

She pulled a pair of leather trousers and a linen shirt off the shelf and placed them on the bed near Kei.

"Whose clothes are they?"

Lorran tensed at the strange tone of his voice. A low growl hummed beneath his words.

"My husband's." She calmly raised her gaze to his and had to suppress a gasp. His eyes glowed like cold, green stones.

"You're married?" He sounded shocked, stunned, almost angry at the thought.

"I'm widowed," she said.

"Who was your husband? You're obviously of the Peer Class. Who was he?" Kei asked, his voice and eyes losing that hardness.

Lorran pushed her shoulders back and stared the king down. "Lord Brennek. My husband was Lord Brennek." She expected him to show some sort of response. Instead he stared at her as if the memory was so minor he couldn't recall it at the moment. Then after long seconds, he nodded.

"I remember him. He decided to fight dragons and got himself bit, first try." Kei slipped on the shirt. "Cronan. Wasn't that the name of the dragon he became?" Kei stopped dressing and looked up. "That's it. That's where I know you. You were in the cave when we went after Cronan." The skin around his eyes tightened as he stared at her. "You stayed with him. Even after the transition, you stayed with him."

"Right until you killed him, yes."

Lorran could hardly believe the words had come from her mouth. Anger, even after five years, still lurked beneath her skin. Anger at this man for killing Brennek before they could save him. Anger at herself for never being able to rescue him.

Kei willed himself not to tense under her fierce gaze. He inserted deliberate casualness into his stance as he stared back at her. This, at least, explained her anger. It didn't, however, explain his response to her. She was pissed and obviously didn't like him much and still the thought of fucking her, of licking her pussy until she whimpered with pleasure, lurked at the edge of all his thoughts. His erection grew and he quickly pulled on the borrowed trousers. It was ironic — here he was a king, ruler of a warrior nation, and he was borrowing the clothes of a man he'd killed.

No, he corrected in his mind. He hadn't killed the man. He'd killed the dragon. He'd have been more than willing to let the man live, annoying though Brennek had been. But not the dragon.

"Cronan was a particularly nasty beast, if I remember correctly. How many women had he captured? Did you keep count?"

Lorran shook her head but kept her lips tightly pressed together.

He was watching her, pushing her. She was angry but still holding back. And he wanted to know why.

"We lost track as well. You say you've studied these creatures. Does it appear that the character of the human is directly related to the irrationality of the beast? I've always wondered if particularly weak-willed humans make better or worse dragons. I'm sure you'd have experience with that."

Her hand came up and Kei prepared for the slap. It never came. She stopped inches from his face and lowered her hand. Her head followed moments later. She was loyal. He had to give her that.

"I apologize, Your Majesty," she said though how the words escaped her tight lips he wasn't sure.

He had the desperate urge to kiss those lips, to taste her and soothe the lines around her mouth. To feel her mouth on him, sucking his cock…Kei inhaled deeply and closed the leathers around his hips. It was a tight fit, particularly since he was sporting an erection that wouldn't release its grip on his cock. He didn't understand it. She was pretty enough. Her face held none of the classically beautiful features. But her eyes were bright with intelligence. Her mahogany hair held brushes of sunlight. Her breasts were full and the nipples perfectly formed, perfect for his mouth. And her cunt…reality faded and all he could think about was tongue fucking her. He licked his lips. Her flavor was gone and he wanted more. *Mine.* The fog invaded the edges of his mind. He walked forward, driven by his carnal urges. She turned away and paced, her arms folded around her waist. He followed her, her words barely making sense.

"Very little is known about the transition and what human elements, if any, remain in the dragon."

The word "dragon" pulled him to a stop. He was right behind her but luckily she hadn't noticed him stalking her. He quickly spun on his heel and stalked back. With his back to her, he adjusted the trousers, easing his hard cock into the supple leather. There was surprisingly enough room. Kei ran his hands down the seam of the leathers. They were custom-made. Either Brennek had been very well endowed, or he'd followed fashion and stuffed his trousers. Either way, it allowed Kei some covering and he wouldn't be straining against the leather.

"The prejudice against dragons is so great," she continued. "If people would simply stop and learn, there might be a way to rescue them."

"Rescue dragons? Why?" Kei couldn't believe what he was hearing. He'd heard about dragon sympathizers before but he'd never met one. And certainly not one whose husband had changed.

"There are places, times, when dragons and humans have lived together in peace."

Kei shook his head. "It's very rare and it's usually after horrendous destruction. The price is too great."

"But we need to learn about them. If we study them, maybe we can stop them from forming. Or reverse it."

He paused and peered at her. "Is that possible? Is there some way to stop it?"

He saw her hesitate. Like she was deciding whether or not to lie. Finally, she took a deep breath. "No. At least not yet. But we need to know more. We need to learn about the transition. What triggers it? Why will a man go along, seemingly recovered from the dragon bite and then in an instant the dragon appears? We need to observe the process."

The dragon trance must have slowed his mental processes down, he decided. *This* was why she was polite when she didn't want to be.

"You want to study me." It wasn't a question. "*Observe* me while I go through this."

"People who study dragons rarely get this opportunity." She hurried across the room. The slow bounce of her breasts caught his attention. In an instant, his thoughts snapped to sucking on her tits. *Damn. What in the Hells is the matter with me?* He forced his mind from lecherous considerations and raised his gaze. "We're always called when a dragon is already formed," she continued. "When the creature is tormenting a town. This is an incredible opportunity. Think of the lives you might save."

She stood before him a strange mix of pride and insecurity. She needed what he could provide but she hated to ask. It was almost as if she was expecting him to reject the idea. And he would. He wasn't about to be studied like some animal in a park.

He had things to do. He had to return to the Castle. *No leave. Mine.*

He shook off the strange thoughts bouncing around his head but couldn't fight the compulsion that drove him to stay. He needed to be near her. Taste her.

"Fine," he said, using the sharp word to drag his thoughts away from fucking her.

"I'm sorry, what?" Her soft brown eyes glowed with a spike of surprise and pleasure.

The muscles along the back of his neck relaxed as if his body was telling him he'd made the right decision.

"I said fine. You can study me."

Chapter 3

Lorran watched as Kei split through another log. Sweat glistened on his bare chest. The hot summer sun was finally setting, turning the sky a dusky pink. Still he continued. He'd been working for hours, almost since his awakening from the trance. Whether it was the strength of the dragon already appearing or Kei's natural energy, she didn't know. At this rate, she'd have more than enough wood for the winter.

He was obviously used to physical labor. His muscles rippled as he lifted the axe and swung it down. Her palms warmed at the memory. She'd spent hours with her hands on his skin, feeling those muscles pulse beneath her fingertips. It had been twelve hours since he'd woken from the trance and twelve hours since she'd touched him. Already she was missing the sensation.

She pressed her hand to her stomach, trying to ease the sudden ache. She gave herself a shake. She had to stop thinking about him in a sexual manner. The strange connection that had been there during the trance was gone. The man was in control, for now. And as the dragon grew, it would distance itself even more. She knew that from experience.

Kei had agreed to stay and allow her to observe him but he knew the truth. There was little chance she'd be able to stop the transition. Some had been able to delay it, but no one had ever succeeded in staying human. Kei drove the axe into the splitting stump and straightened. A light breeze caught his long blond hair and moved it away from his face.

But if it can be done by sheer determination, she thought, Kei is the man who will succeed.

Unfortunately, the dragon was a powerful creature. Having seen the beasts up close, having lived with one, Lorran knew their strength. There was no way a human could defeat one.

Lorran opened the door and approached Kei slowly. They hadn't talked since this morning. Since he'd agreed to let her observe him as he made the change from human to dragon.

"Are you finished?"

Kei nodded. "That should keep you set for awhile."

Lorran looked at the woodpile. "For the next several years I'd imagine."

Kei followed her gaze and she saw the surprise in his eyes as if he'd just realized how much wood he'd actually cut. "I think better when I'm doing something."

"I understand. I—"

"I need to bathe," Kei announced with all the arrogance of a king.

"There's a small tub in the cabin."

Kei raised an eyebrow and stared at her.

"But, that's probably too small," Lorran amended. "There is a waterfall a short distance away. I use it occasionally."

"Do others?"

Kei would be worried about how many others knew he was here. His brother had been concerned about the same thing.

"No. It's too near Effron's lair."

He tensed at the mention of the dragon's name but didn't say anything. Lorran waited. He'd only learned this morning that he would soon turn from king into dragon. She could understand why he needed time to adjust to that concept.

"I'd like to see it," he said quietly.

She knew he meant Effron's lair. After grabbing towels, expecting Kei would want a bath after visiting the dragon's cave, she took him down the south path leading away from her cabin. She'd picked the location for its proximity to the dragon. Effron had killed several cattle and the family dog before the previous owner had moved out.

Everyone in town thought she was insane to live so near to a dragon's lair but if she wanted to study the animal, she needed to be close. She'd walked this path almost daily since moving into the neighborhood a little over a year ago.

Effron was a fairly young dragon. He'd been a foolish nobleman living in the north who'd taken a dare from his friends to sneak into the dragon's lair and search for treasure. The dragon had returned. And this was the result. Another dragon tormenting a new village.

The path twisted around and then began to climb, taking them up the hill to Effron's lair. Kei scanned the forest with every step, a warrior alert for danger.

"Nothing lives in these woods," Lorran said to fill the silence. "Effron's pretty well frightened everything away even though the woods would be fairly safe. Dragons don't hunt in the forest. The trees don't allow free movement of their wings. I think it makes them feel vulnerable. They prefer their prey in the open."

"And close enough to a village so they can terrify humans at the same time."

Lorran decided to let the comment go. She couldn't dispute it. Dragons seemed to delight in destruction. And they had long memories.

They climbed the winding trail in silence. Lorran was used to the steep hill and completed it easily. Kei followed. He wasn't even out of breath when they reached the top. It was almost impossible to believe that three days ago he'd been carried down this mountain battered and bloodied. There was no sign of it now.

They stopped at the crest. Kei surveyed the valley from the rock ledge. Nothing moved down below. She couldn't decide if he was looking for something in the forest, or preparing himself to meet the creature he would soon become. After a moment, he nodded.

"Let's go."

Lorran led the way around the corner. The opening to the cave was small, smaller than it should have been considering it housed a fully grown dragon. Lorran had been there enough times to know the opening expanded into a huge cavern just inside the darkness. Somehow the dragon was able to bend his body to slip through the opening.

Lorran stopped at the entrance. She rarely went inside Effron's lair. She knew how territorial the beasts were and didn't like to intrude.

She glanced at Kei to see how he was taking all of this. The look on his face was grim. Serious and immovable.

The light of his green eyes seemed dim, matching the darkness of the cave.

She wondered what he was thinking. Three days ago he'd walked into this cave to kill a dragon. Now, he was looking at his future.

He stepped inside the cave and waved to Lorran.

"Stay here."

"What?" She stared at him in amazement. "I'm the person who studies dragons. Why would I stay here?"

"He might hurt you."

"He hasn't yet."

Kei paused like he was considering another order. Lorran kept her gaze steady. It went against her childhood training to defy a man, and a king especially, but after the past three days, she found herself ignoring the etiquette she'd learned years ago.

"Fine, but stay back." He turned and walked into the cave.

Lorran shook her head. "I'm not the one he's going to be irritated with. I didn't come after him with a sword," she muttered and followed Kei inside.

The cavern was dark, but sunlight filtered down through crystals so there was enough light once their eyes adjusted. Kei didn't seem to need to wait. He moved in and stopped. The cave was empty. Effron was out. Kei wandered through the open space, his mind obviously caught in its own thoughts. Lorran knew Kei had been inside dragon lairs before, but never looking at it from this angle. The grim lines of his face hardened to stone as he walked the length and breadth of the cave.

He'd said he would suicide rather than allow the dragon to appear. She hadn't wanted to believe it but now looking at him, she knew he was dead serious. There was nothing worse in his mind than turning into one of these creatures.

Kei stared into the pile of metal that characterized the dragon's riches. Lorran knew that it mainly consisted of necklaces broken as they were pulled from women's necks and the various gold buttons from gowns and cloaks. The dragon wasn't interested in wealth but collected items that glittered. Kei bent down, reached into the pile — and pulled out a sword.

His sword. It must have fallen from his hand when the dragon bit him. He inspected the blade and hefted the weapon in his hand as if checking the grip. He rolled his shoulders back and continued to stare at the blank wall.

She had to get him out of there.

"We should go," Lorran announced. "Effron will return soon. He doesn't stay away long." She'd recorded the dragon's habits. It was getting near to dusk. Effron liked to be in his lair before the sun went down. Dragons, though they seemed to have incredible night vision, didn't care for the dark. Even their caves were typically illuminated with some form of crystal.

Kei remained silent but turned to face her. The depths of his eyes glowed with anger and unrepentant hatred for the creatures he'd fought all his life. And for the damage this creature had done to him.

Lorran suddenly felt very ill at ease. She didn't know what would happen but it quickly became clear that Kei and Effron could not meet. Not now.

"Kei, please. Let's go."

Without responding, he turned and walked to the opening.

Lorran stepped into the dying sunlight and froze. They were too late. The heavy flap of wings vibrated the air as they left the cave. A huge gray-green dragon occupied the shelf in front of them. The beast lowered to a crouch and growled low in his throat.

Kei moved beside her, his sword held tight in his hand.

Lorran felt her heart start to pound. Effron ignored her for the most part but she didn't think the dragon would have the same reaction to Kei.

The beast tilted his head and watched them. The black dragon eyes glowed with angry curiosity. He opened his mouth and another growl rumbled through the air. He wasn't happy. Lorran was used to his perusal but this time he ignored her and focused on Kei.

Kei stepped forward, his body compacting into a warrior's stance. The dragon spread his feet wide and bared his teeth.

"Stay behind me," Kei ordered.

"Kei, no."

"Go down the hill, Lorran. I'll take care of him."

"No!" She pulled on Kei's sword arm. He stared at her hand on his elbow and then snapped his gaze to her face.

"What are you doing?"

"Leave him alone."

Effron growled. Kei faced him. And Lorran knew she had to get one of them to back down.

"Kei, please. Don't hurt him. Let's just go."

The dragon shifted its stance as if impatient to begin.

"You can't expect me to walk away."

"I do. We're in his lair. He's protective of his home just as you would be. And to be honest, he's probably not happy to see *you* return with a sword." The dragon raised its massive body up on powerful legs and took two crouching steps toward them. Lorran stepped forward to meet the creature. "Stand very still," Lorran directed.

Kei stared at Lorran's back. She'd placed herself between him and the dragon and now she was giving him orders? He watched and wondered when he'd lost control of the situation.

The answer came quickly. The moment he'd woken inside her cabin.

The dragon continued its slow crawl forward. It reached Lorran. The dragon's mouth opened revealing a row of white, sharp teeth.

"Lorran—" She still had time to back away and then he would move in and destroy the beast. But she waved her hand behind her back indicating he should stay away.

"It's fine. He's done this a number of times." The dragon's snout lowered to her feet and then moved upward, as if he was sniffing her.

A deep growl boiled at the base of Kei's throat. The sound was strangely animalistic. His body reacted without his command, preparing for attack. He couldn't let that beast touch her.

"Kei, slip around behind me and head down the path," Lorran said softly. Her voice startled him. She didn't move. She stood calmly letting the dragon sniff her body. "I'll be fine. Go down the hill."

Everything inside him rebelled. His training and his honor wouldn't allow him to leave Lorran to face a dragon.

But she didn't want it harmed. She would defend the beast.

Kei took a deep breath and did what he'd never done before in his life—he walked away from a righteous battle.

He forced his legs to carry him down the path. It took all his strength. He stopped, just out of sight and watched. The dragon continued his slow perusal of Lorran, inhaling her scent. Kei felt his chest move through a deep breath. He could smell her from the short distance. *Delicious.*

His cock twitched inside the sweaty trousers he wore and he impulsively licked his lips. Hours had passed since he'd been between her legs—the memory a blend of fantasy and fog-covered reality—but he remembered her taste. She was his.

He dug his fingers into the rock wall. His honor as a man and a warrior demanded he move to protect her. Foreign sounds echoed inside his head urging him to steal Lorran away. To keep the beast away from her.

Effron growled and Kei felt his own lips curl back in a snarl to respond. Lorran nodded and began backing slowly away. Kei watched her hips swing softly with each step and instantly imagined the feel of her ass pressed against his hips as he drove inside her. He quickly averted his eyes.

What was wrong with him? He was a king. He was raised to be a gentleman, of a sort. There was no reason to leer at the woman willing to help him.

"Let's go," Lorran said when she reached him. "Effron might decide to come after us. He wasn't in a good mood."

"He talks to you?" Kei was stunned by the idea. No one had ever been able to communicate with the beasts despite the fact that they'd once been human.

"Uh, no. But I've observed him for months now. I know his moods. He wasn't happy at finding you in his lair. Again. Dragons are very territorial."

"What did you promise him?"

The snide question was spoken and Kei immediately realized it had been a mistake.

Lorran's spine straightened and she turned to face him. She glared at him. "Pardon me? What did I *promise* him?"

Her anger seemed to fuel his own. She'd stayed behind and he'd had to walk away. He folded his arms over his chest.

"A dragon's appetites are well known."

"What? You think I agreed to have sex with him simply to get him to leave you alone?"

"There are women who seek out dragons for that purpose."

"I study dragons to help them—not because I'm looking for...because I want..." She folded her arms in a mirror of his own arrogant stance. "It may surprise you, Your Majesty, that Effron has absolutely no interest in me. So, no, I didn't promise him anything except that I would get you to leave. By the Goddesses, you'd think the world revolved around sex. It doesn't. Not even a dragon's world."

With that, she turned on her heel and spun away, stalking down the path toward the loud rush of the waterfall. Kei waited until she was a safe distance away before following. There was something decidedly dangerous about Lorran when she was irritated.

She stood beside the pond at the base of the waterfall waiting as he entered the clearing. She dropped two towels on the rocks.

"Here's the waterfall. Go soak your head."

She started to walk way.

"Lorran, wait. Please." He was momentarily surprised by the penitent sound of his own voice. He couldn't remember the last time he'd said "please" and actually meant it. But he thought Lorran would understand. She would know what it cost him. "I apologize for my comments. I truly do not think you would trade your virtue—" She raised her eyebrows and Kei quickly amended his words. "—your body to the dragon. I was startled that he let you go without harming either of us and I—" This was almost more difficult than the apology but he knew it would be as important. "I appreciate what you did. You placed yourself in front of the dragon so that I could *escape*." He hated that word. It was a cowardly action. "It was very brave of you."

The starch slid from her shoulders. "Effron won't hurt me. He never touches me. He has no interest in me whatsoever."

"But you're a woman." *A lovely, delicious woman with a tasty sex and*—Kei halted the barrage of images. He didn't need any more fuel for the lust-filled thoughts that had haunted him since waking.

"Yes." She chuckled the word but he could hear the pain behind it. "Imagine being the one woman on the planet, it seems, whom the dragons don't want. It does give me a unique opportunity to study them and that's what I've done." She said the words with no emotion but there was more. "I'll leave you to your bath. The cabin is just down the hill."

"Wait. Won't you join me?" The words sounded formal...and totally inappropriate for a king to a noblewoman. "I mean, not join me, of course, but perhaps you'd like to bathe while the opportunity presents itself. Effron is safely in his cave. I'll stand watch. And I promise to look the other direction."

He felt very noble about saying the words. Particularly when what he wanted most was to watch her strip off her ugly gown and walk slowly into the pond, letting the water brush her softly curved thighs, the silky hair between her legs...Kei bit back a groan, the image too real.

"Go. Get in the water. I'll be over there waiting."

He walked to the edge of the rocks that formed the pond and turned, staring into the forest. After a moment, he heard it—the gentle splash as she entered the water. Kei clamped down on sensation, blocking out the sounds of her movements, ignoring the erection that throbbed between his legs. He was a warrior. He wasn't a young boy who couldn't control himself. He would master it.

He listened to the sounds of the forest, hearing only the trees swaying in the winds. Nothing else moved. He held himself still, focusing on the natural world and ignoring the trickle of water as it poured off Lorran's skin. He found he didn't need to see her—his imagination was able to create the picture in his mind quite clearly.

"Kei?" Lorran's voice was soft and tentative. He'd frightened her already. The one person who could help him and he'd frightened her. "Don't—"

He turned and his throat closed. An odd gurgling sound broke from his throat. And suddenly it was very hard to breathe.

She stood before him wrapped in nothing more than a tiny strip of cloth that barely covered her from breast to pussy. Her wet hair hung down around bare shoulders, clinging to her like loving vines. Her long legs were softly curved and strong. He'd watched her ass the entire climb up the mountain so he knew she had strength. He swallowed and tried to clear the lump in his throat and remember that there was a really good reason why he didn't throw her to the ground and fuck her at this moment.

Unfortunately, though he truly believed there was a good reason, he couldn't remember it. He dragged his gaze from the luscious sight of her legs.

She grimaced when he met her eyes, no doubt seeing the obvious lust that had to be visible on his face.

"I was going to say, don't turn around, my dress got wet and I'm almost naked," she said, her voice slightly mocking.

"I'll, uh, go take my bath now." His voice was thin and raspy. Lowering his gaze, Kei forced himself to move by Lorran, the delicious scent of her wet hair almost stopping his steps. He waited by the pond.

He'd woken up beside her—hard. He'd spent the afternoon splitting wood hoping to work off the drive to have her. Nothing seemed capable of killing the raging erection. Each moment that passed, he thought there was no way he could get any harder. And the next moment, he was proven wrong. The only thing keeping his cock from springing high against his stomach was the restriction of his leathers and he wasn't sure the material was going to hold it in much longer.

He had to do something. "It isn't natural," he muttered, as he tore at the ties. "It's not fucking natural to be this fucking hard for this fucking long." He jerked open the trousers and sighed as his cock swung free.

"Your Majesty, are you talking to me?" Lorran's voice came from behind him and a safe distance away. He placed his hands on his hips, disgusted with himself for being unable to control his body in this fashion.

"No, I'm talking to myself." Maybe the cold water would help. He dropped the leathers and stepped out of them and into the pond in one movement. He hit the water. "Dammit." The water wasn't cold. It was warm, almost hot. Perfect.

It was supposed to be uncomfortable. Anything to get his mind off his cock. Lorran's pussy. And her mouth, and her tits, and damn, he had to do something. He dove under the water and swam toward the waterfall. Maybe the pounding would knock him senseless and he could actually survive the next few hours without completely embarrassing himself.

What spark of insanity had made him agree to let her study him as he made the transition? There had been this strange desire, almost a compulsion, to stay with her. And her interest in dragons was the perfect excuse. After he'd agreed, everything seemed normal. He'd never expected to spend the entire time with an erection that wouldn't die.

Kei came out on the back side of the waterfall. He stood waist deep in the pond and let the water pummel his head and shoulders. The sharp stinging bites felt good, just enough pain to keep his body distracted. He grabbed the soap stone and scrubbed his body, brightening his skin with the harsh rock. After his skin glowed and his hair was clean again, he sank into the water, rinsing quickly before rising.

Kei opened his eyes and stared through the waterfall. The sun was almost set but he could see Lorran clearly. She clutched the towel to her chest with one hand and slowly bent to pick up her gown. The movement revealed the curve of her hip, a teasing line of her ass. Kei's mouth began to water. She glanced in his direction as she straightened. She wouldn't be able to see him through the pounding water. She stepped closer to a rock that should have hidden her from his view. Kei moved along behind the falling water, keeping her in sight.

She inched farther behind the rock. An evening wind fluttered the bottom of her towel. Kei caught the scent of her damp flesh as it flowed through the air.

He slipped his hand below the water and touched his shaft. His cock jumped in his palm. He watched, silently begging her to release the towel. He needed to see her. Her full breasts and tight nipples. And her sex. The memory of her flavor floated across his tongue. He pumped his hand along his erection and watched her. Her pussy would be wet. He knew how wet she got from his mouth. He would fill her, drive into her until she would never leave him.

She looked over the edge of the rock to where Kei had stood moments before. The sky was almost dark. She'd never be able to see him. But he could see her.

She turned away. He saw the towel fall to the ground. Her ass was presented before him. She reached up and ran her fingers through the damp strands of her hair.

The strange fog that had haunted his wakening returned. He had to have her.

Silently, almost unconsciously, he moved closer until he stood at the edge of the pond.

Instincts not wholly his own drove him forward. He pushed himself up out of the water. Lorran spun around.

"Wha—" She stepped back but Kei was on her. He silenced her question with his mouth and the sweet flavor of her lips exploded in his senses. Suddenly everything was as it should be. The energy that had flooded his body all day eased and the distant voice in his head faded. He felt her shock but she didn't struggle.

He blocked out all sounds but the whisper of her heart. He molded his lips to hers, and after a moment's hesitation, her softness conceded to his power. She opened for him and he slipped his tongue inside, gently, tempting her to welcome him. As if she knew his desire, she touched the end of his tongue with hers—a light flick that sent too many images through his head of what he wanted that tongue to do. She repeated the caress and he knew she would go where he led.

He sank into the kiss, learning her mouth, her taste, reveling in the tiny whimpers she fed him. He lingered, savoring her flavor, until he was desperate for air. But there was no way he could leave her. He placed light teasing kisses along her jaw line, moving slowly and enjoying every inch of her skin. She tilted her head as he placed his mouth against the sleek column of her neck and her breasts pushed against his chest. He could feel her tight nipples poking him.

He cupped her breasts in his hands and massaged gently, loving the soft moans that fell from her lips. He bent down, latched his mouth to the pert nipple before him and began to suck. The startled gasps of Lorran's pleasure made him shudder in quiet ecstasy. He wanted to give her more—take more—until he consumed her thoughts and desires. Kei swirled his tongue around her nipple and felt it lengthen into his mouth. She arched into him, silently begging for more. He groaned. The dark fog swelled inside his head.

He placed one hand on her ass, keeping her hips connected to his. The tight curls that protected her pussy teased his cock as he eased his length between her thighs. Moisture flowing from her cunt coated his shaft.

Kei bent her back over his other arm, positioning her breasts for his attention. He straightened and looked down. She was stretched out. Displayed before him—her back arched and those delicious mounds thrust upward. His chest rose and fell in shallow pants. He had to have her. He leaned over and placed one gentle, teasing kiss on the curve of her rounded flesh. The desire to overwhelm her in every way clouded his mind. He opened his mouth and laved the hard peak of her breast, relaxing into the luxury of having her before him. He suckled and licked, lingering long until Lorran's cries became desperate. Then he switched his focus to the other breast and gave it the same loving treatment. He smiled against her skin as she twisted and moaned in his arms. She belonged to him. The forest around them disappeared. Only her flavor and desperate sounds were important.

He wanted more. Wanted her begging and screaming his name.

He slid down her body until he knelt before her. Cupping her soft hips in his hands, he lifted one leg over his shoulder until she was open to him. The smell of her arousal swamped him. He moved quickly, hungry for her cunt. In one swift movement, he spread her legs and pushed his face into her hot pussy. She was wet—slippery with her cunt juices. Kei wanted to howl with joy, but wouldn't release the prize of her sex. He sank his tongue inside her and teased the walls of her passage. She shuddered in his arms. The sharp prick of her fingernails on his scalp encouraged him.

He lost track of time—the long hours of daylight faded as he continued to feast on the pussy before him. She squirmed within his hands, silently warning of her climax. He could feel her body start to vibrate. She was coming. He drove his tongue deep inside and rubbed along the top edge of her clit, pushing her, needing her to break the barrier.

"Kei!"

Her cry was new yet still familiar and he drove her onward. She would come. He curled the end of his tongue and felt her body tense.

"By the twelve Goddesses," she gasped.

Kei barely heard the words. The flavor of her skin and the sweet juice she produced at her orgasm was too tempting. He drank from her, knowing from the erratic pulsing of her hips that she was capable of more. It was as if his whole world had centered between her legs.

His cock bounced against his stomach. He needed her. Needed to come inside the tight pussy he'd tasted. Frenzy liked he'd never felt before burned through his veins. He pushed himself to standing. He curled her bent leg around his waist and settled his rock hard shaft against her wet opening. So close. He needed to be inside her.

Mine.

Kei tensed as the foreign voice invaded his thoughts. It came from inside his head, but it didn't belong to him. He recognized it. Scattered dreams from the trance slammed into him—fire and pain and then a gentle cooling. And that voice—always there.

His mind cleared and he felt an invisible band tighten around his chest.

The dragon was alive in his head.

"Kei?" Her lips were swollen from his kisses but her eyes darkened with concern.

He stepped back, knowing he had to distance himself from her. The drive to take her was too strong. If he took her now, he'd be giving control to the beast inside him.

No. Mine.

Need clawed at him from the inside. "I need to fuck you." The words came out a growl. The sound was almost unrecognizable as a human voice.

She stared at him with the dark frightened eyes of prey.

Kei bit his teeth together. The fog was edging out his control. "Kei?" She bent quickly and picked up her dress, holding it in front of her. "What's wrong?" He heard a trace of fear in her voice, but his only thought was that she was hiding herself from him, hiding what belonged to him.

The thought pushed his passion into rage. His lips peeled back in a snarl. Lorran froze at the noise. She stared at him, watching his eyes. Then she began to inch away. He recognized the movement. She was backing away from him as she'd done from Effron.

The image shocked him back into clarity. He stared down at his own body, bent low, preparing to attack.

He forced himself to turn and face the waterfall. What was wrong with him? He'd frightened her. And with good cause.

No!

The voice screamed in his head, urging him on. He could have her. He had to have her. *No leave!*

"Go," he ordered though his throat was tight. He glanced over his shoulder but didn't turn. His cock was so hard and the compulsion to be inside her cunt was still so desperate, he couldn't look at her. "Leave. Now," he said when she hadn't moved.

"Let me help you." Confusion and sympathy surrounded her offer.

She had to leave. He had no chance of controlling the dragon while she was there.

"Just go," he commanded again.

After another moment, while Kei silently begged the Gods to take her away, she started to walk backward. He kept her at the edge of his sight. She waited until she was part way down the path before she turned and hurried away.

When she was safely gone, he stared down the empty trail. The lingering taste of her flesh combined with the bitter taste of disappointment. And anger. She was gone.

He sank to the ground and dropped his head into his hands. Blood burned through his heart. He needed to fuck.

No, he corrected, he needed to fuck her, needed to come inside *her*.

He concentrated on calming his breath and returning his focus to this world. He would get through this. The smell of the cool forest soil momentarily filled his head. Her scent was everywhere inside that little house. There was no way he could go back in there, not in this condition.

With a sigh, he reached down and wrapped his hand around his solid cock. He couldn't have her but he would find his release. He ran his hand from the tip to the base, a quick brush. Her hands would be gentle, delicate fingers teasing his cock. He kept his own touch light, imagining, anticipating her soft skin on his, the warmth of her palm wrapped around his erect cock. He banished the image. He would just do it—get it over with. He had real problems to deal with. He couldn't spend his days battling a massive hard-on.

He tightened his grip and pumped his shaft. He was so hard it wouldn't take much to blow. Pleasure built with each pass of his hand. It shouldn't have taken more than a few strokes but he just grew harder. His climax seemed to move farther out of reach. He squeezed, forming a tight ring with his fingers, moving his hand faster. It only succeeded in increasing the tension. His cock was screaming for release. His whole body vibrated with the need to come.

And he couldn't. He continued. There was no other option. He needed to come.

Inside her.

"No, dammit," he growled to the influence in his mind. He would do this his way.

A spark of awareness stopped his frantic movement. He paused and listened. It was as if something waited just beyond the clearing. He didn't look up. He didn't have to. He knew.

She was watching.

Time and space seemed to no longer apply. He could see her clearly, as if she stood in front of him.

She hadn't returned to the cabin. She'd stayed to watch over him. And now that she'd seen him, seen what he was doing, she'd remained. Kei smiled. His prim little hostess was curious.

No, he couldn't come inside her tonight, but he could come for her. All thoughts of quick relief faded. He rested his shoulders against the rock and tilted his hips sideways to improve her view.

He returned his hand to his cock and began to slowly stroke its length. He lingered, running his palm up and down his shaft, pausing to savor the tension, keeping the movements slow. If Lorran were touching him, he wouldn't rush it. He'd want to enjoy each caress. She'd be soft, tentative, then grow bolder. Her eyes would lighten. Would she enjoy touching him? Something told him she would. She would love the power she had over him — the power to hold him in her spell.

He closed his eyes and pictured her, kneeling beside him, her long lovely fingers stroking him. Knowing she watched, he spread his legs, and began to slowly pump upward, easing his cock into his hand. Soon he would come. But now he wanted to hold off, to know she watched, to imagine her touch. Each stroke of his hand, he pictured Lorran, her full breasts filling his hands, her tight nipples straining for his mouth. He licked his lips. Her pussy, wet for him. She'd torture him with her hands before slowly slipping his shaft inside her cunt. He moaned and pumped his hips faster. She'd hold him tight, her walls clinging to him. And those hot little groans she'd made when he'd touched her. She'd scream when she came.

"Lorran," he whispered through tight teeth as he pumped harder, jacking his hand up and down. He was so close. *Inside her.* He needed to come inside her.

The almost painful need spiraled out of control. There was nothing he could do. He licked his lips, the subtle flavor of her cunt melted on his tongue.

He drove his cock deep into his fist and tensed as his seed poured from him.

* * * * *

Lorran stood in the shadows, just out of sight. She couldn't leave him. Something wasn't right. Though she hadn't spent much time with Brennek during his transition, he hadn't seemed afflicted the way Kei was. The tension that bound his broad shoulders had nothing to do with anger and everything to do with arousal.

Kei was aroused. Around her. She considered the idea that it might be the dragon's influence but it was too soon. He'd only woken from the healing trance that morning.

Through the trees she could see him, his skin bright against the dark rocks, illuminated by the full moon's shining. He dropped his head into his hands like all his energy was gone. Maybe he was looking for an escape—a willing body to lose himself in for a few moments, to forget the horror of the weeks ahead. That had to be it.

Brennek had done the same but it hadn't been her body he'd craved. She would have to find some way of helping Kei. Lorran chewed the edge of her lower lip. She could contact one of the women in the village. There were a few prostitutes that lived openly in town. She could bring one out for Kei.

He shifted, leaning his back against the rock and staring up at the night sky. What was he thinking about? Lorran had only a moment to consider the idea before his movements distracted her. He straightened one leg and bent the other, then he reached down and curled his palm and fingers around the thick length of his cock.

Her breath caught in her throat as he slowly began to slide his hand up the long staff. He was thick, long. And hard. A sudden hollow ache spread through her stomach. Her sex was still damp from Kei's attentions and began to drip. Lorran whimpered.

Kei tensed and for a moment, she was sure he'd heard her but then he relaxed. Surely, he would stop if he thought she was watching. But he continued the steady strokes, even seeming to slow down. The obvious pleasure marked his face as he shifted, twisting his hips until he was fully bared to her now. She could see every line and curve. His thighs strained as he punched his hips upward.

Her breath moved with each thrust, matching his rhythm. He was straining, reaching for his climax. Her own hand curled into a fist. She wanted to touch him, wanted to watch his face as she did exactly what he was doing. His movements grew more frantic as he picked up speed. She couldn't look away. It was beautiful. Her nipples ached. She ran her hand up her body and cupped her breast. She pinched the peak and felt the ache spike between her legs.

He threw his head back. She could hear his groan and watched as white liquid spilled from his fingers.

Alone in the woods, she watched and licked her lips.

Chapter 4

Lorran paced by the window, glancing out, looking for some sign of Kei. He hadn't returned to the cabin last night. After watching him at the waterfall, she'd hurried home and waited, finally falling asleep early in the morning.

The silence was strange. She'd grown used to his presence during his three days in the trance. And sleeping in the bed alone had been uncomfortable. She'd been chased through her sleep with dreams of Kei's hands and lips on her skin. She gripped the edges of her skirt. It was so easy to remember, to re-create the physical memory of his touch. Her sex began to throb, as if preparing for him. She took a deep breath and let her mind drift through her memories—Kei's hand between her legs, his mouth sucking on her pussy, his hand around his own shaft.

She could only imagine what it would feel like—to feel his cock inside her. He'd been thick and long. Her chest grew tight as she struggled to breathe. She unconsciously rolled her hips, a surprising ache between her legs. She sighed and closed her eyes, letting the tension rise. Her nipples rubbed against the soft cotton of her bodice.

She'd been willing last night. If he hadn't pulled away, she would have accepted him into her body. Even now she felt empty, wondering what she had missed.

Though she didn't hear anything, she suddenly knew she was no longer alone. She opened her eyes. Kei waited in the doorway, watching her.

"What were you thinking about, just then?"

She felt a blush tinge her cheeks. "Uh, nothing."

The lines around his eyes deepened but he didn't speak. It was almost as if he could see into her thoughts and knew she'd been daydreaming about him. His long hair was wet. He'd returned to the waterfall this morning. He stared at her for a long moment. She returned his gaze, startled by the wild emotion that flickered in his eyes.

"Are you all right?" she asked, her voice no more than a whisper. He straightened and the strange vulnerability was gone. Something had happened to make him pull back at the waterfall. He'd wanted her. She wiped her damp hands on a dishtowel. "I didn't know what happened to you last night," she said briskly.

"I walked the valley."

Lorran nodded. She didn't know what else to say. "Would you like something to eat?" she asked, desperate for something to do to ease the unusual tension in the room. Kei agreed and within moments Lorran placed a hot meal in front of him. He watched her as she moved around the cabin, his eyes sending streams of heat through her body. She mentally braced herself and collected her parchments before sitting down across from him.

He glanced up but quickly returned his attention to wolfing down his breakfast.

"So, I think we should start." She said opening the paper and inking her quill. "How are you feeling?"

"Fine."

The crisp answer was wholly unenlightening but Lorran noted it. "Do you sense any changes? Any strange thoughts you can't account for?"

His fork stopped halfway to his mouth, then continued. After he swallowed, he shook his head. "No."

Lorran marked down his answer but wasn't sure he was telling the truth.

"We'll need to track your emotions."

"Why?" He finally met her gaze.

"As the dragon's awareness grows, that's where you'll notice changes. Your emotions will intensify. Hatred, anger, pain, humiliation."

"Arousal," he added.

She schooled her expression to show nothing. "Yes, I suppose arousal would be one of the emotions that would appeal to the dragon." She cleared her throat. "Particularly given the dragons' reputation. In that area. But no one has ever reported a transition, during, uh—" She wasn't good at this sort of discussion. Her family hadn't discussed relationships between men and women. Her wedding night had been quite a surprise. "Well, during intimate relations."

"Sex," Kei supplied.

She felt herself blush again. She had to get the conversation back under control. "Yes. Observers have reported that the human begins changing, at least mentally and in their behaviors, long before the dragon physically appears. The person's emotions become very erratic." She kept her voice distant and impersonal. It was strange. She'd never spoken with a man who was going through the process. He appeared so calm about the situation but she'd seen the rage inside. She had no way to ease his anxiety. Though she barely knew him, she dreaded the next weeks. Tears pricked the edges of her eyes.

"What causes the final transition?" he asked. His emotionless voice matched hers. His ability to maintain control inspired hers and Lorran forced the tears to retreat. She sat up in her chair.

"We don't precisely know but it appears these emotions are the gateway. The human—" It helped if she thought of it in general terms instead of the specifics of Kei changing into a dragon. "Displays erratic emotions. Usually building up to an outburst that releases the dragon onto the world."

"And that's when it becomes physically present?"

She nodded. "You'll probably notice the mental awareness much sooner."

"Once the dragon appears, is there any way to return to the human state?"

Lorran was sure he knew the answer but she replied. "No. There has never been a case of a dragon reverting back to a human state."

Kei nodded and thought for a moment before tilting his head to the side. "If emotions are the key, can I keep the dragon away if I succeed in suppressing all emotions?"

"Theoretically," she agreed cautiously. But Lorran felt compelled to tell him the truth. "I've never heard of that working. As the dragon grows, the struggle for control will become more difficult. A few men have succeeded in delaying the transition. But they've been much more mild mannered than…" She let her words trail away.

He put his fork on the table and stared into her eyes.

"Than your average dragon slayer," he said, finishing her sentence with just a touch of mockery.

Lorran couldn't look away. "Exactly." The air between them grew heavy. With just a look, he took her back to the waterfall—the searing sensation of his tongue inside her passage. She shifted in her chair.

Kei's gaze dipped down to her chest, rising and falling with each struggling breath. He swallowed deeply.

"I have to go."

He pushed away from the table and was out the door before Lorran could respond. She stared at his back for a moment before racing after him.

"Kei!" she called. He didn't stop. The moments of sympathy evaporated at his arrogance. He couldn't keep disappearing like this. He'd agreed to her study. "Your Majesty, you can't keep walking away."

He kept moving until he reached the woodpile. He bent and picked up the axe. She wasn't frightened. The man might be a dragon slayer but he wouldn't hurt her.

Lorran followed and stopped between him and the splitting stump. She propped her hands on her hips and glared up at him. Kei stared back, his eyes blazing but with fury not lust. Lorran refused to be intimidated.

"We have more to discuss. I need to get your initial information so we can track the changes."

"We'll do it later."

"If we do it later, I won't know where we started from," she pointed out sensibly.

Kei paused for a second. She watched the muscles along his jaw line tense, like he was holding back a growl.

"We'll do it later," he insisted.

"You've been out of the trance for almost a day and a half and I've been able to observe you for less than three hours."

He leaned on the axe handle and flashed her a smug smile. "But you got an eyeful last night, didn't you? Did you stick around to watch in the name of 'observation'?"

So, he had known she was there. She had two choices. She could blush and stammer or she could respond to his arrogance in kind. She chose the latter.

"It seemed like an opportunity to observe you in your natural state. But I can't monitor your progress if you spend all your time in the forest or breaking logs into splinters! May I point out that you agreed to let me study you and to do that I have to physically see you?"

"Well, may *I* point out that spending the night in the forest was the only option I saw to spending the night here fucking you until you couldn't walk."

His words were like a vise around her throat. She took a short step back.

"W-what?"

"You heard me." Kei let the axe fall to the ground. "You've been through this before. Is it normal? Is this what's supposed to happen? That all I can think about is fucking you and licking your wet little cunt? My Gods help me. I can still taste you and I want more." He stalked forward, stopping directly in front of her. For a moment she thought he would reach for her but he kept his hands clenched at his side. "So, tell me, is this normal?"

Lorran had difficulty finding her voice. She knew his words should have repulsed her but they only succeeded in re-igniting the hunger between her legs. She wanted those things—wanted his cock and his mouth.

"To some extent, yes. Brennek spent his last days in another town with the town women."

"Fucking anything that moved."

Lorran felt her cheeks redden but nodded. "Yes."

"Well then you know what I'm going through so while you might want to observe me, I somehow doubt you're willing to fall into bed and spread your legs in the name of *observation*." He turned around and picked up the axe. His long hair obscured his face as he stared at the ground. "So, until I get this *thing* under control, I suggest you let me work off some of this energy."

Lorran stared at him for a moment and then turned away.

She had no answer for that.

* * * * *

Kei stalked back toward the cabin as the sun began to set. His long hair dripped uncomfortably down his back. He'd returned to the waterfall.

Three baths in twenty-four hours. By the time the dragon appeared, Kei would be exhausted, crazed by sexual frustration, but very clean.

Though it wasn't much, bathing seemed to ease the ache for sex just a little. Nothing worked for long. Everything seemed to inspire thoughts of fucking. And Lorran.

Staying in the forest away from her hadn't helped. Even working himself to exhaustion chopping wood had only dulled the ache for a while. Then something— anything it seemed, a scent, a color, the shape of the axe handle which reminded him of the curve of Lorran's back—would re-ignite the memory and he'd be back hard and desperate.

And he wouldn't find relief any time soon. At least not with Lorran. She'd all but flinched when he'd told her of his desire to fuck her. Unfortunately, while she'd pulled away, his body had leapt in agreement and that thought had occupied hours. Being inside her, riding her pussy until she whimpered with need, until she was totally open to him. Until she was bound to him by unbreakable ties.

He stopped on the porch and waited, hoping his cock would calm down before he went inside. He could have masturbated again but while his body ached with need, the feel of his own hand did little to satisfy it. It only made it worse.

The voice in his head repeated its plaintive cry. *Mine.*

Kei ground his teeth together. The voice was growing in strength if not vocabulary. Even without the words, the beast was pushing him—filling his mind with crisp clear memories of Lorran.

He stared at the door and realized he had only one choice. He had to leave. Had to return to the Castle. Despite what Lorran had said, returning home was the only option now. There were women in the Castle who would welcome him, even eagerly. With a dragon's legendary sexual appetites, there were bound to be a few women who would agree to occupy his bed for the next three weeks. It seemed like the only workable solution. He couldn't stay, not without fucking someone. And the one person he wanted was Lorran.

It had to be proximity. There could be no other reason he was craving her so much. Surely another woman would do.

He opened the door and stopped. The smell of warm fresh bread filled the room making his belly rumble. He welcomed the gnawing pain. It was some feeling besides arousal.

Lorran sat beside the fire, her hands clutching a book but her eyes stared at the flames. She turned as he entered. Concern marred her serene gaze. Dammit—he didn't need her pity.

She slowly rose from her chair.

"Would you like some dinner, Your Majesty?" she asked primly, though she didn't insert the sarcasm into his title this time. Her back was straight and stiff and she looked ready to snap. He waited, preparing himself for another reprimand. Lorran wasn't afraid to speak her mind. He decided he liked that. In the past year, too many people had learned to agree with him—for no other reason than he was king. It was too bad he'd only met Lorran now, when he'd be dead in three weeks. She would have made a wise advisor.

She moved with quick efficiency, brushing past him to the counter without saying a word. Kei wondered for a moment if she'd given up but the tense line of her spine told him she was simply storing up her words. Probably until after he'd eaten.

Her delicious scent combined with the rich smell of the dinner she'd left warming in the oven.

Kei followed her as she placed his dinner on the counter. His cock surged upward. In all the Hells, he'd never imagined a torture quite like this one. He wanted her. All of her. The smell of her pussy added spice to the room, subtle and seductive. He wanted to lick it, taste it.

Drink from it. Pour himself into it until they blended into one being.

There was no way to stop himself. Whether it was the creature that grew inside him or his own natural desire, he didn't question, he simply knew — he had to take at least a taste of what he desperately craved. He gripped her elbow and spun her around, accepting her startled gasp in his mouth. Their lips touched and instantly the ache inside him eased and then exploded. It was sweet and he needed more — he needed all of her.

She seemed to hesitate, but Kei couldn't stop. He drove his tongue inside her mouth, surrounding himself with her flavor. She moaned and he took that as well. He wanted everything she gave. In the corner of his mind he recognized that she wasn't pushing him away, she was accepting him. The world painted itself red in his mind as he settled against her, drawing from her mouth, pulling her body against his, until she cuddled his aching erection between her legs.

Mine.

He circled his hips, pressing against her mound, his body lost in the movements, even if he couldn't yet be inside where he belonged.

Lorran ripped her mouth away, gasping for breath. Kei held her hips and rocked against her. He kissed the column of her neck, distracting her from any chance of clear thought. A brief glimmer of sanity warned she should break the spell. She ignored the warning and sighed as common sense faded.

There was no way to fight the pleasure he gave her. She wanted this. She wanted him. She slid her hands up his chest, needing to hold him. He captured her mouth with his and this time she claimed him in return. She wrapped her arms around his neck. She flicked her tongue against his, mimicking his seductive movements. He groaned, and turned his head, fitting their mouths closer together. He held her hips, almost lifting her as if he wanted inside her body. She'd never been needed like this.

Fucking you until you couldn't walk.

The memory of his words and sharp admission fired the ache between her legs. Her nipples peaked against the soft material of her chemise. Unable to resist, she rubbed against his chest, loving the light friction. Kei pulled one hand impatiently away from her ass and slipped it down the front of her dress, quickly tearing the ties away. His hot palm cupped her breast, holding the heavy weight, while he scattered kisses across her jaw.

"Kei," she sighed, the word a quiet plea—for more of the turmoil he was creating inside her.

He straightened. Lorran blinked at the sudden loss of his mouth. His eyes glowed as he stared at the curves of her breasts visible through the opening of her bodice. With deliberate hands, he spread the edges of material wide and displayed her naked breasts.

Lorran waited, her eyes watching his, searching for some reaction. Her husband had liked her breasts but had never stared at them with the fascination Kei was showing now. He reached out one long finger and trailed it along the curve of her breast, circling closer until finally he traced the pink outline of her tight nipple. The peak pushed out farther, as if reaching for his touch.

"Beautiful," he said as he bent and attached his mouth to her straining nipple. He bit down gently, then eased the pressure with soft gentle pulls of his mouth. A lightning bolt connected her breast to her sex. She squirmed in his grasp as the emptiness between her legs grew more pronounced.

He eased his thigh forward, pressing into the space, moving against her aching pussy. She sighed and tentatively pushed against him. Kei groaned into her skin and the sound echoed through her body, each rumble of pleasure he released sending another caress deep in the center of her body. She settled her weight down on his leg, curling her ankle around the back of his calf to hold him in place. The empty ache turned into anticipation. She pressed against his thigh feeling the sweet pain of her rising orgasm.

Reaching down, he cupped her hips and lifted her off her feet. The world turned as he spun around and carried her the short distance across the room. He sat her on the table's edge and flipped her skirts out of the way. In one fluid move, he pulled her hips forward and settled his covered cock against her pussy.

He hitched his hips forward and positioned his erection along her slit, massaging with subtle pulses. Lorran gasped and dragged his mouth back to hers, luring his tongue inside.

After long desperate kisses, he pulled back.

"You're wet for me." He put his hand between them cupping her dripping sex, slipping the tip of his finger into her passage. "Your cunt is flowing all this juice just for me." He nibbled her earlobe. "Now, I'm going to drink from you."

"Yes!"

At her cry, Kei dropped to his knees. With no prelude, he spread her lips, clamped his mouth over her sex and began to lick. He seemed desperate for her. Lorran leaned back, spreading her arms wide and clutching the far side of the table to keep her body upright. Her hips tilted forward opening her wider to Kei's touch. The light flutter of his tongue drove shivers deep into her stomach. Her head suddenly seemed too heavy. His eagerness and hungry feasting was wildly seductive. He licked the length of her sex and swirled his tongue around her clit, teasing the sensitive nub. The wet, ravishing caress sent violent shudders through her body.

"Kei!" Her body continued to pulse, recovering from the sharp sparkling climax. But still she wanted more. She slid her hips forward, unconsciously opening herself to him. He took full advantage.

His tongue slid into her cunt, slipping deep into her passage as if to gather as much of her juice as possible.

Spots formed in front of her eyes and Lorran felt her arms weaken. She fell backward on the table and stared up at the ceiling, trying to keep coherent thoughts somewhere in her mind. She would lose her sanity if she gave into this blinding pleasure.

But there was no chance to pull away. Kei wouldn't let her. His initial hunger seemingly eased, he slowed his movements, sipping and licking, pulling softly on her lower lips. But his lingering kisses did nothing to slow the fire burning in her. It only intensified the heat. Long, sensuous moments passed. Lorran twisted within the grip of his strong hands. The pleasure was almost painful and the need so great she could barely speak to plead with him. He flicked his tongue over her clit and she whimpered. It was too much.

"Please, Kei, no more."

He ignored the protest and pushed his tongue into her sex. The warm liquid turned to gold on his tongue and he wanted more, wanted all of it. All of her. His fingers tightened compulsively on her thighs, holding her in place for the sweet invasion of his mouth.

He drove his tongue into her again, her cries blending with the voice in his head. He had to have more of her. He curled the end of his tongue, wanting to get deeper. She struggled, smashing her cunt against his mouth. He rewarded her need by sucking softly on her clit. Then he stretched two fingers inside her cunt—reaching what his tongue could not. He traced the inner walls of her tight passage. Her cry pierced the sensual fog that surrounded him and he raised his head. She was flat on the table, legs spread wide, her dress rucked up—and she didn't seem to notice. Her mind was lost in what he'd done to her.

He dropped his eyes back to her naked pussy. "Mine," he whispered. He didn't know where the sentiment came from, only that it was true.

He returned his mouth to her cunt and placed light kisses across her sex, savoring her scent and flavor, reveling in the soft moans she made. The strange haze still hovered at the edges of his mind. His own desires were simply heightened by the dragon's cravings. He couldn't stop it, couldn't slow the need to taste her.

This was where he belonged—forever between her legs. The creature's silent voice rumbled in his head, encouraging him, urging him on. More, and more still. The sweet liquid that flowed between her thighs belonged to him.

He pushed her again and again to climax. Her pleas became cries then whimpers, then threats and then returned to desperate pleas. The desire to fuck her grew with each orgasm.

He slipped one long finger into her pussy and growled. *Mine.* He wanted it. Wanted to shove his cock inside her, fill her with his come.

"Fuck you," he muttered through clenched teeth.

She blinked rapidly and lifted her head inches off the table. The blurred look in her eyes faded as she focused.

"I need to fuck you." His voice sounded foreign but the need drove him on. She was open to him—he could take what he needed but he wanted her acceptance, her agreement that she desired this as much as he did. He waited. Emotions not wholly his own welled up—anger, pain and resignation multiplying inside him with each passing moment.

Take her. Take her. Kei fought the urge, knowing it was from a source outside himself—from the desperate voice inside his head.

"Yes."

The word was soft but distinct. Kei gripped the edge of the table, forcing himself to remain still despite the desire to pounce. She watched him with a clear, direct stare.

He couldn't resist one more taste. He trailed his tongue up the length of her pussy, savoring the flavor.

The beast inside urged him on—the prospect of filling her was too tempting. Kei stood up.

Lorran stared at him, questions filling her eyes, curiosity and concern. She took a deep breath and he watched reality return to her gaze. The languid sensuality that had mellowed her body was replaced by a forced relaxation. He could almost see her mind work—as if she were cataloging each action.

She wouldn't turn this into some experiment. By the Hells, he wouldn't let her do that.

He took her hips in his hands and pulled her off the table. With three quick tugs, he stripped the dress off her body. She stood before him—eyes lowered. He could tell she wanted to cover herself—hide from his scrutiny—but she held still. She was lovely—large firm breasts with nipples that hungered for his mouth, a gentle indent at her waist and the soft flare of her curved hips. He'd hold those hips as he drove deep into her.

"Turn around," he commanded. Her eyes widened in confusion and Kei had a fleeting thought about how unimaginative her previous lovers had been. He had much to teach her.

After a long moment, she slowly turned. He gently pushed her forward until her hands were flat against the tabletop.

"Kei?" She looked over her shoulder, her eyes questioning.

He wrapped his arm around her waist and pressed his hips against hers.

"Don't worry, sweet," he whispered in her ear. "I can fill you from here." He cupped her bare pussy and slipped the tip of one finger inside, just enough to remind her where he belonged. The sharp intake of her breath told him she wasn't the distant observer she'd imagined herself.

Her bare ass glowed beneath his palm. He rubbed his hand across the smooth flesh. She fit him perfectly.

"I'll be so deep inside your cunt—" His voice was soft and low. "I'll become a part of you. You'll never lose the feel of me. You'll want me inside you always."

She pushed up on her hands, gasping for breath.

Kei wrenched the ties at the top of his borrowed trousers, the pressure of his cock pushing the strings wide. He shoved the leathers down and moved against her. She was soft, her skin a whisper of silk along his.

"Can you feel me?" He kept his lips against her ear, his voice soft, for her alone. She nodded. "I'm going to fill you, come inside you until you can't take any more, until you're dripping with my come." She shivered in his arms and rocked her hips onto his teasing fingers. She was ready for him.

Her hands curled into fists on the tabletop as he spread her legs and pushed the tip of his cock into her entrance.

She tensed. He was thick and stretched her passage with the first inch he moved into her. "Shh. Relax, sweet, let me have this pussy. It's mine. Let me have it."

She let his words flow through her and she found the courage to release her muscles. More of his shaft slid inside. He moved slowly, supplying her with one slow heavy inch after another. Her body adjusted, molding around his shaft. He paused as if giving her time to learn him. And then there was more. She thought he'd never end. Finally, his hips were pressed against her and he was deep inside.

She could feel him. Heat flowing from his cock spread through her body, warming the darkest corners. His soft voice whispered comforting nonsense about her beauty and how delicious she felt. She rested back, settling against him. It seemed to be the sign he needed. He began to move.

The long slow pull out of her pussy seemed to go on forever. She vaguely recognized the strange panting sounds as coming from her but nothing she did seemed to stop them.

"Do you like that, sweet?" His words were hot against her ear. He nipped at the edge of her lobe, layering the sensation upon the unrelenting thrust of his cock back into her pussy. One thick arm was wrapped around her waist, holding her hips steady for his invasion. The other hand cupped the heavy weight of one breast. "Do you?"

With each question, he pressed a little deeper, starting again the delectable torment. The orgasms of moments past faded and a new line of arousal began. Lorran took long, deep breaths, trying to fight the surge that coursed through her. Nothing had ever felt like this. Except her dreams.

"Kei." She meant it as a protest. It came out as a plea.

"That's it, pretty one. Gods, your pussy is so tight. You hold me so close. Like you never want to let me go." He pulled her back, until she was almost standing. He canted his hips forward, staying inside her. He massaged the full mounds of her breasts. His warmth flowed from his skin, heating her inside.

She dropped her head back against his shoulder as her breath left her lips in ragged gasps.

"Tell me, Lorran. Does it feel good? Do you like my cock inside you?"

She couldn't stand it any more. "Yes!"

"Shall I give you more?" He bent her forward, inching his thick length ever so slightly deeper into her passage.

She was gone. Pride was gone. She wanted what Kei could give her, all that he could give her. Nothing had ever felt this desperate.

"Yes," she whimpered. "Please."

Without speaking, Kei straightened and grasped her hips with both hands. She reached forward to grab the edge of the table and supported her weight. When she was bent all the way forward, he shoved deep into her—hard. The long seductive moves were gone, leaving behind the hard deep thrusts.

"Aaah." Her cry resonated in the tiny cabin. It wasn't pain—it was need, pleasure. "Yes, yes!" she moaned, her words timed to the hard pounding into her pussy. He slid in deep and stopped. Her mind screamed in protest. She was so close. The sweet tightening that warned her climax was near vibrated through her body. She just needed a little more. She pushed back, trying to slide him deeper, guide his cock where she needed it. His strong hands held her still. She was at his mercy and he wasn't done tormenting her yet. Slowly, the long line of his cock pulled out, almost leaving her body. "Noo. Please, Kei."

"Hold still."

"No, Kei, I need you." She hated the pleading sound of her voice but he couldn't stop now.

"You need this." He punched his cock into her one time. "That's what you need." His large palm ran down the length of her bare back. "Don't worry, sweet. It's yours. I'll give you all the cock you need. And you'll give me this sweet pussy, right?" He pulled out and held himself at her entrance.

"Kei!"

"Won't you?" he demanded. "Give me all the pussy I need? All I want?" He gave her a slight taste, pushing a thick inch back inside. She whimpered, squeezing her lips together to crush the sound. "Tell me," he urged.

"Yes. All the pussy you want, all that you need."

Triumph and surrender blended in his growl of approval.

Kei took a deep breath, drawing in the scent of her arousal. It was strong, powerful. He pushed forward, sliding inch by inch into the wet pussy that begged for his rod. A masculine power like he'd never felt before came over him. His mate, bent forward and pleading for his cock. Her tiny gasping breaths reached his ears and the soft whimper as he settled himself once again full hilt into her passage.

He struggled to keep his movements slow, fighting the animal in his head that drove him to pound into her—that screamed for a hard fast fuck—repeatedly filling her with his cock.

The long slide into her pussy was a sweet torture all its own. He pushed himself to the hilt and held there, enjoying the feel of her wet walls around his cock.

This was it. This was what had teased him since his awakening. He didn't know what called him but he belonged inside her body.

He arched his hips, moving in a tiny circle within her body.

She gasped. Kei smiled.
Mine.

"Please, Kei."

"Beg me, sweet." He didn't know where the deep need for her cries came from but he wanted it. "Beg me to fuck this sweet cunt." He rolled his hips in a long slow swirl, teasing her with more of what she needed.

"Yes, fuck me. Please." He didn't move. "Oh Goddesses, Kei! Fuck my cunt. Fuck me." Her voice was ragged and pleading.

He knew the words were unfamiliar and crude to her but he loved the desperation. He loved knowing she needed him so much she would put aside her inhibitions to plead for his cock.

He could do nothing else but give her what she begged for. His body exploded from the mental restraint. He entered her over and over, hard, fast, deep. She braced her arms against the table and pushed back, countering his thrusts, fucking herself onto his cock. "Fuck me. Please, Kei, fuck me. More, please, give me more, fill me."

"All you want."

Then he, and the dragon raging inside him, fucked the woman. She was tight and sweet. The more he drove into her, the more he wanted of her. Her moisture flowed over his hand still massaging the soft skin between her legs. She had to be sensitive—he circled the outer edge of her clit.

Her cries rang through his ears. Her incoherent begging was littered with his name. She called to him, demanding he satisfy her. His own body screamed for completion but he couldn't let her go before she'd come with his cock inside her. He cupped her pussy and drove in hard, forcing her clit against his palm and sending his shaft deep into her cunt. Her back straightened and her body tensed. Soft fluttering caresses teased his cock as her pussy contracted with her climax. He roared and filled her one last time, flooding her with his seed.

Kei held himself still as all strength drained his body.

They both sank to the table. After a long moment, he pushed up onto his elbows, relieving her of some of his weight. But he couldn't leave her body. Not yet. He held his hips firmly against her, keeping his cock deep inside her.

He listened to the sounds of their breathing.

He'd never fucked like that before—or come that hard. And it stayed in his thoughts—each thrust, each sensation ran through his mind—replayed. He felt his cock harden inside her. Impossible. He couldn't recover that quickly. Lorran whimpered as he grew inside her.

"Kei?" Her voice sounded worried.

He should leave her. He'd used her hard already. But he couldn't convince his body to respond. It felt like he'd been waiting forever to be inside her.

"Shh, shh. Slow and soft," he promised, feeling none of the impending desire to drive himself into her pussy. Just the lovely feel of her cunt. He straightened and settled his hips behind hers. He pulsed deep inside her. Her passage clung to him, trying to hold him in place.

Lorran blinked and stared into the fire, feeling the slow throb of arousal. Her body was exhausted but she couldn't fight the tingling pleasure. It was just as he promised—slow and soft. Short thrusts deep inside, massaging her inner walls. The rise to climax flowed through her body. It was a long steady climb.

She had no idea how long she lay there, flat against the table while Kei fucked her from behind. She only knew the tension built slowly to an unbearable level, until she begged for him to let her come.

He adjusted, giving her the deep caress she needed. Release built through her body, long and deep, just like his loving.

"Mine," he whispered as he poured himself into her for a second time.

* * * * *

In the early morning hours, Lorran lay in bed, staring into the darkness. The weight of Kei's arm was heavy around her waist, holding her back to his front. Her heart was slowly returning to normal. Kei was asleep. Her body was exhausted but her mind raced with possibilities. And reality.

What had happened tonight? By the pale light of the triple moons shining in the window, she could make out the lines of her dining table. Would she ever be able to look at it again without thinking of Kei bending her over it, riding her hard and long? The steady rhythm of her heart increased at the thought, when her body should be sated.

Her husband had come to her bed on a consistent basis, until it was clear she was barren. Then he'd taken his pleasure with the women in town. After Brennek had left her bed, she'd missed the physical contact and the gentle orgasms she'd reached.

None of it could compare to the feeling of Kei inside her body.

Even now, her body quickened, looking for more of the delicious sensations. It was impossible. She'd lost track of the times she'd climaxed. Kei had carried her to the bed and mounted her again and yet again. She pressed her lips together, crushing the whimper that threatened. Her body was sore but beyond the slight pain was the need—she wanted him inside her.

"Hmm?" Kei shifted behind her, rubbing his chest against her back and pulling her more tightly against his hips. The rough brush of the hair on his thighs scraped the backs of her legs. Lorran took a deep breath, hoping to calm her rapid heartbeat. It didn't work.

Kei's hand slid downward and brushed lightly against the top edge of her bush. He stroked the pale hair, lazily running his fingers through the curls. Almost unconsciously, Lorran tilted her hips forward, trying to catch the tips of his fingers, wanting to guide his random strokes.

"More?"

The word was mumbled into her hair. She didn't know if Kei was asleep or awake but it didn't matter. He reached around and slowly turned her until she faced him. His hand slid down the outside of her thigh and pulled her leg forward, opening her pussy to him. In a drowsy movement that seemed to last forever, he slid his hard cock inside her sex. Lorran tensed for a moment, the thick length still new to her body. As the penetration was completed, she relaxed, the aching need gone.

Slow short pulses rocked his shaft into her cunt—soft and sweet, as if he needed the connection between them as well. His hand slipped down and met the point where their bodies were joined. There was no move to make her come—just the union of their bodies.

Kei pulled her head down to his chest and seemed to settle deeper into sleep.

What would he think when he woke up the next morning? Would he look at her in disgust? Would he remember? Had somehow the dragon already begun to influence his behavior? It didn't make sense. None of the dragons she'd studied had shown any sexual interest in her. No, there had to be another explanation.

It was probably the same drive that had sent Brennek to the village girls while his transition lasted. Her eyes began to droop. And she vaguely acknowledged that she was drifting to sleep with her questions unanswered—and Kei's cock buried inside her.

She awoke to the sound of her own groan and the thrust of Kei's shaft into her. Her eyes popped open. He was above her, watching her intently as he drove into her pussy.

The heat in his eyes was marred by a hint of something else—pain? Fear? At what? The dragon? Her rejection? She didn't know. She only knew she wanted to banish it. She curled her legs up, wrapping her ankles around his waist. She used the leverage to pull him deeper. His eyes widened for a fraction of a second and she was satisfied by his sharp intake of breath. He pulled slowly back, as if savoring the clinging of her walls to each inch of his cock. His eyes still drilled into hers, he pushed in deep. Her body rushed to accommodate him but it was still tight. She wiggled, trying to take him deeper. She wanted it all—more of what he'd given her last night. His strength, his power, his seed. Everything that he offered—that he needed to give—she wanted.

"More?" Kei growled, interrupting her scattered thoughts. "You'll give me more pussy?"

He asked softly but she heard the pain, and answered.

"Yes, Kei. All that you want, all that you need."

Chapter 5

She could never have imagined how those words would haunt her in the days that followed. He'd asked for access to her body and she'd given it—willingly. Often.

Lorran looked down at her body—her breasts were bare, the edge of her gown clinging to her nipples, a last bit of modesty. She didn't know why she bothered. Kei would have her naked and spread in moments.

He'd seduced her with so much more than his touch. He'd talked and listened. And fucked her. She squirmed as the simple word invoked the complex memories of his mouth and tongue, cock and hands, him filling her body. She groaned silently and relaxed on the bed.

In her more self-deluding moments, she was almost able to convince herself that she'd allowed his attentions to ease his need for sex. To keep him comfortable while he made the transition.

With her body empty and aching to be filled, she knew it was a lie. In four days, she'd become addicted to the pleasure he could provide. She'd gone from modest to wanton.

His prediction had come true. She'd learned to crave the feel of him inside her. She would never lose the sensation, the thick throbbing length of his cock in her pussy.

And worse—she'd never lose the memory of him in her life. She didn't know how it had happened but she was learning the man. He was much more than a warrior or a king who ruled a nation. He'd become her companion, working around the cabin, filling the day hours between mounting her and doing odd jobs, building furniture, sealing gaps in the logs.

He'd somehow fit himself into her life.

It was not a good idea, she acknowledged. She couldn't grow to care about him, either as a man or a dragon. It was too risky. She knew Kei's future and it didn't include her.

His future was a ragged life in a rock cave creating havoc until someone found the strength to destroy him.

She took a long breath and looked at the situation with stone cold distance. Kei liked having sex with her. She liked it with him. They would leave it at that. She'd separate her observations from their physical relationship. She would keep her distance. It wouldn't do to fall in—she stopped herself before she could even think the word.

With a groan, she closed her eyes and let her head fall back on the pillow. Could she do it? She just had to focus on the pleasure he gave her. It wasn't difficult. There was no way to escape the memories in this cabin. The sights and smells would forever remind her of Kei's touch and the feel of him. She shifted around on the bed, cognizant of her solitude.

"What are you thinking about?"

She opened her eyes. He'd returned from the waterfall and waited beside the bed, fucking her with his eyes.

"You." The breathless honesty of her answer seemed to please him.

"Tell me."

Lorran's first reaction was to refuse. She still hadn't grown used to the words or the power of his attraction. Then she looked into his eyes. He was fighting his demon tonight. He stared intently, waiting for her.

Lorran inhaled deeply and tried to speak her desire. "I was imagining you inside me, hard and thrusting." The words sent physical memories through her body. She raised her arms over her head and closed her eyes as the dream took her. "You're so thick and fill me so deep. Over and over you slide into me. Hmmm. More," she sighed.

"Is that what you want?" Kei's voice dropped to a deep gravelly sound. "A hard fuck? From me?"

Lorran opened her eyes and smiled. Power and seduction flowed in her veins. She could make this man want her—something she'd never imagined before. "Yes. A *long*, hard fuck."

She held his gaze while she reached down and pulled her nightgown up. She watched his eyes. They started to glow then turned almost black as she lifted the material above her waist. She bent her knees and spread her thighs. Her fingers teased the top edge of curls protecting her femininity. Kei licked his lips and stared at her sex, his eyes captured by the sight.

"I love your mouth," she whispered. His body tensed. "The way you lick my pussy, taste me. The way you push your tongue inside me." A shiver moved over her body and she moaned. "It's so good."

She never saw him move. He was beside her, on top of her, his hands flung the rest of her skirt out of the way and his mouth was hot against her cunt before she could react.

He covered her sex with his mouth and eased his tongue deep inside. Lorran cried out and grabbed the back of his head. He licked the supple lining of her flesh, teasing her, tasting her until she could only gasp and beg. And she did, filling the room with her cries, her pleas for more.

The first climax slammed into her body. This was what he gave her — the constant pleasure. And the need for more.

"Oh, Kei, more. Please."

He growled as he moved up her body and Lorran opened her arms to welcome him.

"Inside me. Please, come inside me."

She watched his eyes flare and then he was there, hard and deep and filling her.

"Oh, yes. Kei, that's so good." Words tumbled from her mouth as he began to move. Every thrust he went deeper, as if he wanted to climb into her body, become a part of her. She watched his eyes. The dragon was growing stronger.

The idea made her tense. Kei pushed in to the hilt of his shaft and held himself there, stretching her tight passage.

She stared into his eyes and was struck by the pain. The beast was on him tonight. Lorran reached up and smoothed her hand down his cheek.

"I need you tonight," he whispered. It was a plea and the need came from a place she couldn't understand. But she couldn't leave him to ache like this.

"Yes," she replied.

* * * * *

The bleak light returned to Kei's eyes the next morning. In the cold dawn, there was no way for her to comfort him. And he didn't seek her comfort now. He knew his destiny as well as she did.

After cleaning the cabin and watching Kei stalk into the forest, Lorran decided to walk to town. She needed the time to herself and she was out of some staple items.

Lorran lifted her chin as she walked into the General Store about an hour later. The glares that were sent her direction were not new. She'd grown used to the disdain of the townspeople. But today it was different.

Always before she'd been able to ignore their taunts, knowing she had righteous virtue on her side. But now, it was true.

She'd become the dragon's lover. Dragon's whore is what they'd call her.

He'd been relentless last night, pushing her ever higher and himself ever deeper as if trying to banish the darkness with her body. Her legs ached. Her pussy throbbed from the constant pounding. And more was the memory of her own voice begging him to fuck her, to come inside her. She blushed as the door closed behind her.

"Mistress Lorran, welcome." The storeowner, Mr. Fiya greeted her with a friendly smile. Many in town didn't approve of his serving her. They wanted her to leave and hoped if she were unable to purchase goods, she would do so. He'd shrugged and welcomed her anyway. Fiya owned the only store in town so few could afford not to patronize his shop.

"Mr. Fiya," she said.

"It's been awhile since you've been by. I bet you're desperate for some fresh flour."

"I am." She followed him around the small store, dismissing the small group of women who gathered to stare at her. It was a stare designed to intimidate. Most days, Lorran had no problem ignoring them but today, she felt decidedly conspicuous.

"Humph," one woman grunted as Lorran passed by. The woman led the crowd as they pointedly turned their backs to Lorran. The situation suddenly seemed so ridiculous. These women didn't understand. They never would.

Lorran squeezed her lips together and resisted the urge to open her arms wide and shout, "Yes, I'm fucking a dragon and it's incredible."

Fiya gathered her order and placed the items in a rough cloth sack.

"Now, Mistress, you be careful on the walk home," he warned. "Effron's been particularly nasty these last few days. Don't know what's got him so riled up."

Another dragon in the neighborhood. Lorran kept the comment to herself. No one knew about Kei and it had to stay that way. Riker had somehow managed to keep it a secret. Kei still sent and received daily messages from the Castle. He gave instructions to his advisors and commanders but only provided vague assurances of his recovery and imminent return. She didn't understand it but she had a feeling there was someone at the Castle he didn't trust. She didn't think it was Riker. Kei spoke of him with great fondness. There had to be someone else.

"Dragon whore." The hissed comment snapped Lorran from her thoughts. She raised her eyes and stared defiantly at the women crowded at the back of the store.

Mr. Fiya placed a comforting hand on her shoulder. "Don't let them get to you," he whispered. "You just keep on doing what you're doing."

Lorran nodded and walked out. *And what am I doing?*

That question haunted her as she walked home. The past week had changed her. She'd gone from an observer to a participant. Even now, she couldn't believe the things she'd done with Kei. When they'd started, she never realized the danger. The obvious danger of living with a man about to take on dragon form had proven easy to endure. No, the true danger had been to her heart, during those quiet moments after the loving, when Kei held her in his arms and told her of his plans for the kingdom; or those meals when Kei listened intently as she discussed her research; or the long hours when he loved her body, whispering hot sexy words and showing her how desirable she was.

She was falling in love with him. Her steps slowed as she left the town and started down the path to her cabin. In love. With a dragon. This was what she'd feared last night.

Dammit, she couldn't do it again. She hadn't been *in love* with her husband but that would make this time so much worse. The pain as Brennek had turned from her, as the dragon Cronan had ignored her presence, was an ever present wound. She'd tolerated it because she'd committed herself to Brennek. And because she felt responsible for his change.

But how much worse would it be when Kei changed—when he turned from her, not wanting her touch. When he stepped around her to reach for a woman he'd kidnapped from the village. Her throat tightened and she swallowed deeply, trying to dislodge the lump that had formed.

She had to stop it. Somehow. She had to step back. She'd lost her ability to observe, involved herself too deeply in the subject. The few others who studied dragons as she did had warned her not to get involved. She had to remain separate—apart from the victim. Sympathy only led to pain. Dragon's rarely lived for long and they made rotten friends.

This time, she'd let herself get involved with the human but the result would be the same.

She pressed her shoulders down. Well, she'd just have to get herself uninvolved. How hard could it be? She would keep her discussions with Kei strictly to learning how the dragon was impacting him. And she wouldn't watch him as he split wood or worked in the garden. She wouldn't wait for his reaction to dinner to see if she'd pleased him in some small way.

She could do it, she silently vowed. In the interest of her own sanity, she could pull herself away from the Kei.

Until nighttime. Then, what was she going to do? Each night as they ate dinner, his eyes would begin to warm and with a word or a slight tug of his hand, he would lure her into passion.

It didn't take much to get her into his arms. Just the hint of fire in his gaze. He'd watch her, pierce her with those hot eyes as if he wanted to look away but couldn't.

She'd fight the pull, until the pressure became too much and they'd fly together, desperate to be united.

Her body ached from the constant assault, but still she wanted more. The simple heat of his gaze sent a sharp pain to the center of her stomach, a need to feel him inside her. Even now, with only the memory to warm her, her sex began to moisten, to open, readying for his penetration.

She stopped and leaned against a tree, waiting for the sensation to pass and her knees to strengthen. Well, if nothing else came from this, she had memories to draw from for years to come. Somehow she knew, Kei would be the standard for all other men.

She quietly growled as she pushed herself away from the tree. It was a strange habit she'd learned from Kei over the past days — growling when she wasn't happy. It seemed to work for him. When she did it, he just laughed. But when she was alone it made her feel better, more powerful.

She savored that power, trying to remember it as she walked into the clearing. Kei was at his usual position, splintering logs into tiny slivers — trying to exhaust the demon in his head.

He looked up as she approached the cabin. His nostrils flared like a wild animal scenting his mate. He started toward her, then stopped. The tight line of his jaw was the only sign of any response. He was fighting, struggling against another of those demons.

She would tell him her decision tonight. It was best for everyone. She knew it and Kei would see the logic of it.

She waited until dinner was on the table. And this time she brought her parchment and quill with her.

"So, I'm a little behind on recording my observations. I thought I should catch up."

Kei looked up but didn't speak.

"I've made notes about the progress of our studies so far. I just need your input." She cleared her throat. "Are you noticing a change in your..." She looked down and saw his plate. "Uh, appetite?"

Kei straightened in his chair and stared at her. Lorran lifted her chin and returned the gaze. She couldn't let herself be intimidated. Or seduced. She had to protect what was left of her heart. Kei's eyes crinkled at the edges as if he were trying to figure out what she was up to. Damn the man was too perceptive by half.

"Kei?" she prompted. "Changes in your appetite?" He seemed to enjoy whatever she cooked. He'd been raised a warrior before becoming a king—no doubt he was used to worse food.

Finally he shook his head but his eyes didn't lose the wariness.

"Ability to sleep?" Again he shook his head. "Do you feel the dragon's presence growing in you?"

He paused as if considering his answer then said, "No."

"Is there anything unusual about your behavior? Anything that you notice is different from before the bite?" She pressed her shoulders back and tapped her quill on the edge of the paper. "I didn't know you before so I don't know if there is any personality change that's occurred."

"You mean besides the constant need to fuck?" he growled.

Lorran swallowed. "Uh, yes."

"No, that's pretty much the only the change."

"What do you attribute the, uhm... constant need to..." She'd said the words before, usually shouting them as Kei was entering her body, but to sit and discuss it calmly... "Engage in sexual relations?"

The corner of his mouth kicked up in a smirk.

"Kei?" she pressed when he didn't answer. His lips flattened out.

"I don't know."

"Really?" She let her skepticism creep into her voice. He was hesitating too much between answers. He was either lying or not telling her everything.

He pushed back from the table and stood. He grabbed his plate and walked to the sink before speaking. "What? You want me to tell you that the dragon is talking to me? Fine. He's in my head, or my body, or some damn place. He's just there and all he wants to do is fuck. Trust me, that's the only thing going through the creature's mind."

Lorran cleared her throat. "Dragons are known to have rapacious sexual appetites."

"This one does, and lucky for me, we've found a woman willing to accommodate us."

"Well, since you brought that up, I think we have come to the end of that portion of our relationship."

She waited for the growl, or grumble, or sigh, or some sort of response. He was silent. Finally, she lifted her head and met his eyes. They were cold green stones.

"What?" His voice was soft and menacing when he spoke.

It was infinitely worse than a shout or growl.

"I think we need to stop our intimate encounters," she reasserted. She folded her hands primly on the table, planning to calmly lay out the logic that had brought her to this point. "We've been together every night—" *and day*, she added silently, "since you awoke from the trance. The dragon has not appeared. We have to conclude that while there is some need for sex, it is not something that brings about the transition into the dragon. And I believe that we must move on."

She waited, defiantly meeting Kei's stare. She wouldn't back down on this. Kei already meant too much to her. She had to begin distancing herself from him. His eyes seemed to darken as they watched her. He pushed himself away from the counter.

"Fucking me was just an experiment?" The chill in his voice sent a shiver down Lorran's back.

She didn't dare lie to him. "Well, no, but we must use all the knowledge that we can gather. And we have to take into consideration that our, uh, physical relationship might be encouraging the dragon's presence."

"So, it becomes stronger because we fuck?" He didn't sound like he believed it and she couldn't really blame him. But any excuse would do. She couldn't tell him the truth. *I could easily fall in love with you.*

"I think it's something we need to consider," she said primly, marking a note in her pad.

"Very well," he agreed, his voice quiet and unconcerned. "If that's what you would like." He wandered across the room.

"There is a cot in the closet," Lorran said, hoping to keep her voice as equally disinterested. She thought she'd succeeded quite well.

"Of course. I'll set that up."

No, he definitely sounded more casual about it. As she cleared the table and washed the dishes, she grumbled under her breath.

She'd expected him to escape—to head toward the woodpile and continue his campaign to decimate the forest. Instead, he collected the cot and set it up on the opposite side of the cabin. Then he sat down in front of the fire, ignoring her.

"He could have at least protested a little," she muttered as she scrubbed the stew pot. Obviously, she'd made the right decision. Their hours together had come to mean too much to her and they meant nothing more than an available body to him. There was the possibility that the need for sex would drive him into town but she had to believe he'd return. If for no other reason than he'd said he would allow her observation.

She finished the dishes and turned around. Kei continued to watch the fire. It was strange to work without his scrutiny. Every other night, he'd watched her, lust becoming a palpable sensation in the room.

She studied him for a moment. His jaw was tight and his knuckles white. He was fighting something. She wanted to ask him about it—but the need to comfort him was too great. She couldn't. Though it killed her inside, she turned away. She had to protect herself. Her life had been thrown into turmoil when her husband had made the change into a dragon. The guilt and regret that lingered from that experience still weighed on her heart. How much worse would it be this time, when her heart was engaged? There was only one way for her to survive this time—she had to build the distance between herself and Kei.

"I'm going to bed," she announced, though it was early. There was no reason to stay awake and they needed to adapt to this new routine. Kei nodded but didn't look up.

Lorran pulled the curtain around the bed, isolating it from the rest of the cabin. The fire glowed behind the material. She took a deep breath and pulled a sleeping gown from the closet. Her nipples poked up against the light cotton material as she drew it over her head. Unable to resist, she cupped her breasts and rubbed her fingers across the tight peaks, remembering the heat of Kei's hands and the wet warmth of his mouth sucking her.

It only served to increase the ever present hunger between her legs.

With a deep breath, she dropped her hands and willed herself to ignore the ache. She crawled onto the bed and stared at the ceiling, her body humming with need. A long time later, she heard Kei bank the fire and move across the cabin. She blinked away silly tears that threatened because he wasn't climbing into her bed. She had to focus on the future. And that meant banishing Kei now.

She closed her eyes, determined to fall asleep. She would sleep, she *wouldn't* think about Kei and she wouldn't think about how empty she felt.

She would learn to do without him.

* * * * *

Kei stared at the curtain and emitted a low, predatory growl.

He crushed the sound. It was too much like the growls and snarls of the beast that clawed at his insides. He wasn't that beast. He never would be.

He rolled over onto his back and stared up at the ceiling.

It was a nice sentiment but it wasn't true. He would turn into the beast.

Lorran said no one had ever been able to stop the transition. Some claimed to have slowed it but in the end, he would turn into the creature. The thought didn't frighten him perhaps as much as it should. The end was moving closer. He just had to maintain his sanity for a while longer, keep the beast at bay. Kei drew in a deep breath, expanding his chest and holding it. As the breath escaped, he relaxed and allowed himself to drift into a light sleep.

The rustle of cloth against cloth snapped his mind awake and his body immediately began to harden. She was near, just on the other side of a thin slice of material. Unable to resist, he looked across the room, trying to penetrate the curtain. His night vision had always been good but now, the room looked no darker than morning. The dragon's instincts and abilities were starting to show.

He'd have to tell Lorran. She'd write it down and make that humming noise she made when she turned new information over in her quick little mind. It was a softer version of the groan she released when he entered her warm body.

He'd grown used to the strangled pleas that broke from her mouth. It made him want to push harder, deeper—push her until she couldn't hold anything back, until she would give him everything. Then she made the most delicious sounds, the tiny gasps turned to screams and demands that he fuck her.

His hand slipped across the skin of his stomach to the hard erection that pressed up against the single blanket he used. His flesh jumped at the first touch of his own hand.

Mine.

He wanted her, needed her. His fingers slid up the hard length, pretending it was her hand. He bit back a low moan. It was so easy to recall the light touch of her fingers on his cock and a shudder ran through his body. He grew even harder. Why was he tormenting himself like this? He couldn't come this way. Not once he'd been inside her pussy. He'd tried, those first few nights when he'd been driven to mount Lorran over and over again. Unwilling to use her in such a fashion, he'd tried to satisfy his lust alone but though he stayed hard, nothing but Lorran's touch could bring him to climax. That was another little tidbit he hadn't shared with her. He probably should. She'd find it interesting.

Interesting. That's all he was to her. An experiment and maybe a charity case.

And now she considered the experiment completed. Unable to stop the sound this time, he growled toward the curtain. She thought she could block him out. For almost a week he'd slept beside her, loved her body. He'd held himself inside her, felt her wrapped around his cock, holding him. And tonight she'd put a wall between them.

Mine.

The word pulsed through his head.

Mine.

He moved, rolling out of the bed and starting toward her sleeping alcove. She belonged to him. The urge was overwhelming. As he neared, the sweet scent of her pussy reached him. Kei stopped for a moment. He absorbed the lovely smell and licked his lips, remembering the alluring taste.

His hand landed on the curtain, ready to tear it open, rip it down, and crawl over her, plunge inside her.

Yes, the beast urged. *Mine.*

Kei felt the control of his body fade.

He jerked back the partition. Lorran's eyes snapped open as she lay curled on her side. In a brief moment of clarity, he realized she hadn't been asleep—there was no disorientation from being suddenly woken, but even as the thought came to him, it was replaced by a hunger that crushed rationality. Instinct ruled and his instincts told him she belonged to him. The line between his urges and the dragon's blended and at this moment he couldn't tell who was in charge—just that he needed her, needed to be inside her.

The dark haze that perpetually lurked in his mind swamped him as he stared down at Lorran. The crisp sharp senses of the dragon picked up every nuance of her skin, the soft curve of her cheek, the plump swell of her breasts.

She rolled onto her back and moved like she was going to sit up. Her eyes glowed with unasked questions.

Kei watched as if from a distance, feeling the dragon's desires break free inside.

The woman was there. He could smell her, almost taste her.

He crawled onto the bed, adapting to the strange musculature of this human body. The faint memory of her taste and the soft clasp of her sex around his tongue drove him forward. He placed one hand on either side of her hips and straddled her. She would be wet and waiting.

Lorran stared up as Kei crouched over her, his movements slow and deliberate, as if the muscles and bones were alien shapes.

"Kei?"

He slowly swung his head left then right.

Nekane.

The word entered her mind, never crossing Kei's lips. The voice was deep and gravelly.

"Nekane," she repeated.

The dragon had a name.

Chapter 6

She reached out, placing her hand on his chest.

"Kei," she called again.

The light press of her fingers on his skin combined with her soft voice and eased the dragon's grip on his mind. He tensed. His first reaction was to back away, to tell her not to touch him. The desire was too close to the surface and his control was thin. This was a need beyond the desire to fuck—he wanted to possess her, consume her, climb inside her until she could never escape.

She moved toward him. She was closer now. "Take a deep breath. Fight it. Don't let him win." She whispered to him. The words blurred, barely distinguishable, but the sound of her voice soothed the rough edges of control. She was near. That's what he needed. He took a deep breath and inhaled her warm scent. Her hair hung down around her shoulders wild from the press of the pillows.

He lost track of where the dragon's needs ended and his began. He only knew he needed her. She could keep the fog at bay—she could hold him to this earth. Kei pulled Lorran to him, covered her mouth with his own. Her taste entered him like an arrow, sharp and clear— opening his heart. The tiny gasps and groans he'd craved earlier were his reward as he sank his tongue in the wet warmth of her mouth. She met him, her own tongue tangling with his.

Through the haze of desire he realized she was accepting him, welcoming him. The dragon drew back but didn't disappear. Kei could feel him, hovering just beyond this world. Images and flavors flooded his mind as the dragon urged him on with memories of her cunt, the full mounds of her breasts.

Kei slid his hands around her back and pulled her hard against his body. The hard line of his erection was pressed against the wet slit of her sex. Through the thin material of her nightgown, he could feel her moisture. The beast roared inside him, as if knowing that she hungered for him pleased the creature. Kei clenched his teeth, trying to maintain control but the sights and smells of Lorran's passion along with the dragon's influence pushed him to the edge. He had to have her.

Lorran gasped as Kei moved. His strong hands spread her thighs and scooped her forward. The heavy weight of their bodies tilted them backward onto the cushion of the bed. He ripped the long line of her nightgown. The high neck tore in his hands baring her breasts. She only had a moment to react before his hands covered the soft mounds.

"I need you."

The hopeless glint in his eyes called to her. She opened her legs. He looked down, staring at her thighs spread open before him. He drew in a sharp, tense breath.

"Come inside me."

Immediately, he was there—plunging deep, ravaging her pussy. She was wet but the deep sudden penetration stung. She bit her lips together to hide the startled gasp that threatened. She wanted this, wanted to ease him with her body. Her passage quickly adjusted to his entrance and grew wet, openly accepting him inside.

Lorran held him, whispering softly as he thrust into her. She ran her hands along his shoulders and chest, loving the tension in his strong muscles as he moved above her. Each time he'd pulled back, her cunt would tighten, clinging to him, wanting to hold him. Wordless pleas slipped from her lips, the need for more, the need to feel him deeper inside her.

"Mine." The word slipped from his mouth almost unnoticed. As much as she'd tried to reject it, she couldn't. He needed her. At least for now, he needed the comfort of her body, and she couldn't deny him what he needed.

Her heart throbbed deep in her throat. No one had ever truly *needed* her before.

"Yes," she agreed. "Whatever you need." She knew she was committing herself to him, even if he didn't understand.

"I need you. I need this pussy."

"Yes—all that you need." She repeated her vow from the first night.

Kei growled and seemed to swell inside her. Lorran fell back on the bed. He was hard between her legs, pumping into her with the strength of a madman.

He slid home and Lorran gasped.

Kei pulled out, stopping at the rim of her sex, as if he knew he should stop but couldn't bear to leave the warmth of her cunt.

"I'm hurting you."

"No." She wrapped her legs around his waist and pulled him down, using her strength to slide his cock back inside her, back where he belonged. "Please Kei. Fuck me. Please."

His eyes grew dark and he reared up before thrusting forward again and again. He held nothing back, giving her all of his strength and power as he slammed his cock into her. She lost her ability to speak or even think coherently. Her last clear thought was it was too late—she'd given her body and her heart to a dragon.

* * * * *

Kei silently paced the far side of the room, stopping every few steps to stare at Lorran's sleeping form. He'd dragged himself out of the bed knowing if he stayed beside her, she'd never get any rest. He couldn't seem to stop. The urges that had moved through him before seemed minor to the overwhelming desire to stay inside her. In the Dark Hells, what had he done to her tonight?

Everything. Anything.

And she'd allowed it.

Or maybe she hadn't. He hadn't given her much opportunity to protest. She'd been frightened when the dragon had pounced on her but she'd helped him control the beast—and in return, he'd fucked her to oblivion, using her body to ease the fierce ache.

What had he done?

The creature was getting stronger. There was no doubt about that now.

Kei walked the length of the cabin. Even now, after hours of fucking, he wanted her. The jutting spike of his cock was evidence of that. From across the room, he could track her, smell the sweet scent of her arousal.

There was so much he hadn't told her. How his eyesight was better, his sense of smell stronger. He'd kept those secrets back. There was so much he *should* tell her, but saying the words aloud made it too real. The beast was growing in him.

Nekane.

He tensed at the mental growl, recognizing it as the voice of his urges. He closed his eyes and willed the creature away. He was still strong enough that the beast quieted after a few moments.

Kei shook his head. Would this be what his life would be like until the end? Voices in his head and a rock hard cock?

Tonight brought his death one step closer. He couldn't wait much longer to return to the Castle. He would not allow himself to become a dragon, a beast that terrorized the people he'd spent his life protecting. He would ask Riker to kill him. He hated leaving his death on his brother's young shoulders but the dragon was rising quickly.

He looked at Lorran.

Dragons had long memories. If the unimaginable happened and Kei made the transition, would the dragon come back for her? There was only one way to protect her—he had to take her back to the Castle. Riker would look after her, guard her. Kei took a deep breath. Maybe then, she'd drop this strange obsession with dragons. It was going to get her killed.

And by the Gods, he didn't want to be the dragon who did it. He knew that once the change took place he'd be unaware of anything but his own rage, but there was the fear, the lingering dread that the human being he'd been would recognize her and mourn her loss.

"Kei?" Lorran's sleepy voice was like a spike into his soul. "Come back to bed." And the woman who a week ago would have flinched at the thought of walking around without petticoats, pulled back the blankets and bared her body to him. "I need you," she muttered, her eyes drooping closed. She spread her legs. "Inside me."

Kei tried to resist the call but who could resist the lure of a beautiful, naked woman opening her legs and asking for him? He stumbled across the room. There was no lingering foreplay, no teasing caresses. He simply slid his erection inside her pussy.

Still half asleep, Lorran smiled and sighed, seemingly comforted to have his cock inside her body. She wrapped her legs around his waist and snuggled him up tight.

She dropped her head back onto the pillow and relaxed. Kei couldn't stop the mocking smile.

His little prude was asleep, content only to sleep with a cock buried deep inside her. What would she do when he was gone? In the past week, he'd spent so much time inside her, he wasn't sure she'd be able to survive without it. He would tell Riker to come up with a suitable list of possible husbands for her.

The dragon roared in his head. And Kei's mind went black.

When he came back to himself, what he thought was moments later, he found his body thrusting deep into Lorran's. She was fully awake now, panting, begging.

"Please, Kei, oh yes, please. Kei!"

Her fingernails digging in his shoulders and the dreamy, dazed look in her eyes told him he hadn't hurt her during the time when he'd been gone. He couldn't stop himself, couldn't deny her. She needed it. So did the beast inside him.

Bind her, keep her. Mine.

His mind was clear; his body was under the dragon's control. Kei could only follow where the beast sent him, thrusting deeper and longer into her cunt. Lorran's sweet moans and pleas drove him on. She was wet and hungry for him. She gasped and arched up against him. The now familiar contractions of her orgasm massaged his cock and Kei groaned. He thrust several times more, drawing every bit of pleasure from her. Then, he let his body go and released his seed into her depths.

Long moments of glowing oblivion passed before he found the strength to push himself up on his arms. He stared down at the sated woman in his arms. Her legs were still wrapped around his back, like she wanted to keep him inside her. Her eyes fluttered open and her lips curled into a dreamy smile. She didn't understand. Kei felt the pounding of his own heart increase.

Nekane had been in control.

Did she know it?

Was Lorran even aware she'd been fucking a dragon?

* * * * *

Kei climbed out of the bed in the early morning hours. The dragon growled as Kei pulled his cock from Lorran's pussy. Her forehead crinkled as if she was irritated at being disturbed. Then she fell back into a deep, sated sleep.

The moment of masculine arrogance couldn't be ignored. He'd done that to her—taught her to crave his cock as much as he longed for her pussy. His erection grew as he watched her on the bed, but he dismissed it and dressed in the borrowed leathers, situating his hard cock inside the pouch.

Kei walked outside without knowing where he was going—only that he needed to be moving—to think about the night before. The dragon was there, in his mind. Kei could feel him. Where before it had been a strange hovering presence, now the creature seemed to take up a portion of his mind. Tales of the erratic behavior of men before their final transitions made more sense now. The dragon invaded the brain, taking it over in increments until it was strong enough to control the body—then it would appear in its full corporeal form.

Kei stopped and stared down at the empty valley, realizing he'd climbed to Effron's lair without knowing it. The canopy of trees covered Lorran's cabin. The village was in the opposite direction. Smoke curled from chimneys half obscured by trees. This was the perfect place for a dragon's lair—isolated yet within reach of those he meant to torment.

Kei turned and stared at the cave entrance. The dragon was inside. Kei could sense him. He could smell the other creature and hear the quiet swish of scales across the stone walls as the dragon moved in the cave.

He took a deep breath and walked inside. There was no need to adjust to the lack of light. His heightened senses allowed him to see every crack in the stone walls and every scale of the dragon's hide.

Effron consumed the space, sitting back on his haunches and snaking his long neck forward. Kei stood just inside the entrance, giving the dragon a moment to get used to his presence. Effron tilted his head to the side and stared for a moment, then turned away, dismissing Kei.

The anger and rage that Kei associated with dragons was there. He'd seen it often when he'd hunted the creatures. But now Kei recognized something else. Beneath the fury was pain—isolation—an overwhelming feeling of loneliness.

The dragon was a solitary creature, destined to remain alone because of his nature. Kei felt the awareness of the beast in his head grow. Its anger and denial at Effron's state throbbing through Kei's skull.

Mine.

The dragon in Kei's head whispered the word as if to remind him of Lorran. Effron raised his head and growled.

Kei stilled as the dragon rose up on his legs. Once again he'd come to the cave without a weapon. He wasn't afraid. Just as now he understood the dragon's loneliness, he also knew Effron recognized him as a similar creature. Kei folded his arms and watched the dragon pull his head back, open his mouth and exhale. Flames burst from deep in Effron's throat. The fire flowed over Kei.

He tensed, waiting for the pain. But there was none.

The flames didn't burn him.

Effron growled and sent another wave of fire over Kei. Then he hunkered down in the corner and turned his head away.

Kei watched for a moment longer. The dragon fire didn't burn him. He'd been singed often enough in the past that it was a novel experience to feel the flames but have no damage done. The only explanation was the dragon inside him. Effron had sent the flame as a warning.

He wanted Kei gone. Kei nodded to himself and walked away. He didn't want to add to the creature's pain.

As he stepped into the sunlight, the weight of Effron's solitude hung on Kei's shoulders and began to settle into his heart. This was his future.

Mine.

The insistent cry of the dragon seemed to reach across the valley but Kei knew it was only in his mind.

Mine!

The beast was calling for Lorran.

She was waiting for him. She'd helped him soothe the creature last night. She could push away the isolation. Kei stared unseeing at the valley. It would be so easy to rely on her. To do what he'd done last night and bury his pain in her sweet flesh. She would help him. Her sympathy for the dragon would drive her even if affection for him did not.

He couldn't do it. He would fight this and face it alone.

He started down the hillside—away from Lorran's cabin.

* * * * *

Lorran folded her arms across her chest. The slight breeze slipped through the thin material of her gown. She really should go inside and get a shawl but she couldn't. No, not with *her* inside.

It was the perfect plan. Well, perfect might not be the right word. It was appropriate. Smart. She knew Kei's need for sex and she would supply him with it.

Kei hadn't returned last night or through the long hours of daylight. He'd climbed out of her bed yesterday morning and disappeared into the forest. She didn't worry that he was hurt. Not only was he "Kei the Dragon Slayer," but he was now a dragon's host. Nothing that lived in this forest could harm him.

She knew why he hadn't returned. He was running from the demons in his mind — trying to out-run, out-race reality. Nekane's appearance had become a direct reminder of what Kei faced. But he would return. Kei would keep his promise to her to let her observe him. Not even a dragon could stop him.

Lorran sighed. She hadn't been prepared for Nekane's appearance in her bedroom two nights ago. It seemed too soon for the dragon to be this developed. Obviously, there were things Kei hadn't told her about the dragon's presence.

Nekane.

Shivers raced down her arms. The gravelly whisper of the dragon's name echoed in her memory. He'd been close but Kei had been able to conquer him. But for how long?

The man in question finally walked out of the woods and headed across the clearing. The grim lines of his face told her he'd accepted his fate. He was a warrior and, more importantly, a king.

He knew when to face the truth, even when it was painful.

The taut line of his body begged for the comfort of her touch but as he approached she backed away.

Even in the pale light of a single moon she could see the green of his eyes darken. She held herself steady. He would understand in a moment.

"What's wrong?" The ice that covered his voice was tainted by a hint of rage lurking beneath. This was why she had to follow through. The dragon needed to be soothed.

"Nothing," she answered quickly.

His eyes squinted as he stared at her. "What are you doing out here? It's cold. Come inside." He stepped onto the porch and moved toward the door. Lorran shook her head.

"You go. I'll be in later." Much later, she added silently.

Kei cocked his head to the side but didn't ask the question she could see in his eyes. He didn't have to say the words. She knew she was acting strangely. She was amazed at the unusual tension that hung between them. In their short time together, they'd learned to move in unison. Now she was pulling away.

Kei didn't understand. But he would.

She turned away and stared out at the darkening sky, hoping he would take the hint and go inside. It had to start. Start so it could end.

The quiet click of the door closing behind him sent a stab of pain into her heart. It was all well and good to tell herself that it was for the best, but in the silence of the night, she knew the truth. She hated the thought of sharing him with another woman.

She listened to the silence then realized she hadn't thought very far ahead. She had nowhere to go. She'd have to walk the yard until it was over and she could move back into the warmth of the house. She'd—

"What in the Hells is this?" Kei's shout reverberated from inside.

Lorran winced and turned to face the cabin, mentally preparing herself for his appearance. The front door swung open and crashed against the cabin wall in perfect punctuation to his words.

Fury and rage glowed not only from his eyes but vibrated through his body. She swallowed deeply and tightened her fists.

"What do you mean?" she asked as casually as she could.

"Who is that?"

"Her name is Maka, and she's a—a—a girl from the village."

"She's a whore from the village. What the fuck is she doing here?"

Lorran pushed her shoulders back and stared up into his eyes. "She's here for you."

"Just two nights ago, you agreed to give me all I needed. Now, you're backing out."

"No."

"Then I don't want her."

"I can't, you know…" Years of training stalled her from saying the words. "I can't…have relations with you right now."

"Have relations? Is that a fancy way to say fuck? You won't fuck me, is that what you're saying?" He was angry. And maybe a little hurt.

"I can't." The distinction was clear in her mind. "It's my woman's time." Her voice automatically dropped to a whisper. "After the other night when you, and Nekane—" Kei flinched at the name of his future self, but Lorran continued. "Were denied sex, I didn't want a repeat of the incident. I can't—" Kei's glare made her stop. She placed her fists on her hips and glared right back at him. "I can't fuck you right now, so I got someone who could. I thought it best to keep things smooth and calm."

"You just found someone and I'm supposed to mount them."

Lorran folded her arms over her chest. She knew the life of a nobleman. "And you've never been with a stranger before?" Her husband had had so many women there was no way he could have known all their names.

"Yes, but *I* chose them. They weren't picked out by my current lover." Kei crossed his arms on his chest. She could have sworn he was pouting. "Send her away."

"But—"

"I won't have her. Send her away."

The corners of Lorran's mouth tightened but she turned and stalked into the cabin. Kei waited until she was gone and released his pent up breath.

What was happening to him? The woman, Maka, had stood before him, naked. Her tight luscious body welcoming him. It would have been an evening of simple, mindless fucking. And he couldn't.

His mind acknowledged her beauty from a distance. Her form had been long and sleek. The type of woman he liked. Even her eyes had widened with a curious desire. She might have been paid to be here but she was intrigued by fucking a dragon. She wanted to know if the legends were true—if a dragon really could fuck all night long and still want more.

He could have assured her—the legends were definitely true. He'd spent hours between Lorran's thighs and desired more. He wanted her now. But she couldn't take him tonight.

He would never admit it to Lorran, but bringing a whore from the town *was* a logical solution.

But the woman had stood before him and he'd had no desire for her. No desire to make her moan or bring her pleasure. No desire to even take his own pleasure on her.

Simply put, she wasn't Lorran.

He swiped his blond hair back over the top of his head.

It was something else he could never tell Lorran.

The door opened behind him and the woman from town walked out. Her hips swayed from side to side with deliberate seduction.

"One last chance?" she offered.

Kei shook his head.

"Well, a girl can try." She winked as she walked away.

He saw the tiny bag of coins she held in her hand. By its weight, she'd been well paid for no services.

He watched until she disappeared into the trees. She'd be safe on the short walk to town. A dragon in the neighborhood kept bandits away.

When she was gone, Kei drew in a deep breath of air and walked into the cabin. Lorran tidied the room, acting like the strange woman had never been there. Kei could still smell her. The light perfume of Lorran mixed with the drugging scent of the other woman.

"I prepared your cot," she said with an efficiency born of nerves.

"No."

She raised her eyes. Defiance glared back at him.

"I told you—"

"I know what you told me. I won't touch you, if that's what you want, but I will sleep next to you." He didn't look too closely at his motives. He only knew he wanted and needed to be near her. Even if it was fully clothed and sexless. Something akin to pain threatened each time he thought about being separated from her.

"But—" The thought that she was rejecting him flashed into his mind and the creature inside him rumbled. The sound echoed in the room. Kei jerked back and Lorran flinched.

"Was that…Nekane?"

Kei nodded. The creature had sent mental messages but never a verbal noise.

"Well, now we know he can make sounds."

"And that he's irritated at the thought of you sleeping alone."

"Right. The *dragon's* irritated." She sounded a little annoyed herself but didn't say anything else. She nodded. "Fine. We'll both sleep here." She indicated the alcove that had served as their shared bed. "It makes sense, of course. No need for one of us to sleep on the uncomfortable cot when there is a perfectly good bed." She straightened her spine and smoothed her skirt.

She was stiff and strained but underneath it, he saw a tiny glimmer of relief.

Kei kept his distance through dinner and as they worked companionably to clean up. Years traveling with a band of warriors had taught him to clean up after himself. Lorran seemed pleased with the assistance and it gave him an excuse to be near her—even if he couldn't touch her.

As the final evening light disappeared and cradled the world in darkness, Kei tossed down the towel he'd used to dry the plates.

"Are you ready for bed?"

Lorran tensed at the seductive tone of his voice. She'd been on the verge of screaming all night. First, with the prostitute in her house, then Kei's rejection of her seemingly "perfect" plan, which she didn't understand, and now this—all night, he'd lingered near, never touching but never letting her out of arms reach. It was like a seduction with no possibility of a climax. Overall, quite frustrating.

She started to protest.

"Come to bed," he said. He didn't touch her or pull her toward the sleeping alcove. He simply turned away, leading her in the direction he wanted. He pulled off the heavy shirt he wore and hung it over the edge of the chair. Lorran felt the responding flicker in her heart at the sight of his bare chest. She wanted to touch him, feel him. Her breath stuck in her throat as his hands dropped to the waistband of his leathers. With a few notable exceptions, she hadn't spent much time watching Kei undress. Their clothes usually got torn off in a haphazard fashion while they were straining for each other's bodies.

She watched as he opened the flap of his trousers and shoved the soft leather down his strong, powerful legs. When he straightened, he looked up at her and smiled. She barely noticed the smile, so intent as she was on the erection that stood from the nest of pale hair between his thighs.

"It's late. Come to bed." This time, there was a command to his words, a sound Lorran's body couldn't resist.

She stopped by the bed and changed quickly into a soft flannel gown. She turned her back to Kei but the attempt at modesty was wasted. She could feel his gaze on her skin, a hot caress that warmed the center of her body.

Embarrassed, keeping her eyes lowered, she turned and climbed under the blankets. Kei's warm body met hers and molded to her shape without words. She tensed waiting for him to begin touching her in a sexual way but while his touch was sensual, it wasn't seeking. He cuddled her close and snuggled into the blankets, like a child holding his favorite toy.

"Kei—" She didn't really know what she was going to say. She found no will to protest. It felt too wonderful to be wrapped in his arms this way.

"Hush, sweet. It's late. We're both exhausted and sunrise is early."

She looked at his face. His eyes were closed and a slight contented smile lingered on his mouth. What more could she do? She relaxed down onto his chest and moments later drifted off into a dream-filled sleep.

Kei felt the moment she succumbed to slumber. His mind and body were screaming yet strangely content. He didn't understand the beast inside his head. The creature's comprehension was extremely limited. He wanted to fuck Lorran. That much Kei could tell. But having been denied the pleasure of her cunt, the dragon seemed content, as long as Lorran stayed near. It was when she moved away that the beast grew agitated.

Kei opened his eyes and stared into the darkness. Or what should have been darkness. Every item in the room was visible. The ever-increasing dragon senses made him aware of the normally invisible world. A mouse scurried under the larder door, searching for bits of food. Lorran wasn't going to like that. He'd set some traps in the morning. She kept a clean house but the forest nearby made it a constant battle.

Go.

The little creature lifted his head as if he heard Kei's mental command. *Go,* he repeated with a mental push. The mouse spun around and raced to the door. Kei chuckled softly in the dark.

Lorran stirred. "What?" Her sleepy eyes blinked open.

"Nothing, sweet, go back to sleep."

She nodded and rested back on his chest. She settled herself and her hand slipped down until she held his hard shaft in her palm.

Kei tensed and waited but Lorran's breathing slowed to deep sleep. By the Gods, she was doing this to torture him. He was in for a long night.

* * * * *

Lorran woke up as she always did when the sun peeked through the window. She was warm and comfortable. As she opened her eyes and re-gathered her wits, she saw why—she was practically on top of Kei. She smiled up at him. He glowered back. The darkening of his eyes wasn't from the dragon's presence.

Kei—the human—was upset.

Tense.

"What's wrong?"

"Be very careful how you move your hand," he ordered, his voice strung like a wire.

"Why?" She asked the question, and then realized where her hand was—wrapped around his cock.

And from the look of it, it had been there awhile.

She felt her lips curl upward. "Poor baby," she teased. "This looks uncomfortable. How about if I do this?" She slid her hand up the line of his staff. Kei groaned. "Oh? You didn't like that? What about this?" She tightened her grip and retraced the path. His hips thrust upward, forcing his erection through her palm.

"You little witch," he growled through clenched teeth.

"Do you want me to stop?" She kept her movements light, just the flicker of her fingers, avoiding the hard pumps she knew would finish him off quickly. She pushed the blankets further back and stared at him. His cock stood proudly before her. She was intimately acquainted with it inside her but she decided then and there she hadn't spent nearly enough time exploring it. She ran her fingers lightly across the smooth, hard shaft. Finally, unable to resist, she leaned forward and placed a light kiss on the tip.

Kei made a choking sound she'd never heard him make before. She glanced up. His eyes were closed, squeezed tight as his body stretched beneath her touch. He wanted this, had maybe hungered for it but he'd never asked. She opened her mouth and flicked her tongue against his skin—just a taste, enough to capture the warm masculine flavor.

"Have you ever taken a man's cock in your mouth?" he asked, his voice strained.

She didn't answer him but the image tempted her. She'd heard tales of course. The maids had talked about pleasuring their men that way, but she'd never considered it. Until now.

He opened his eyes and watched her intently, his gaze darkening with lust and the strength of the dragon. She reached up and ran her fingertips down the center of his chest, tracing the taut muscles that held him bound to her. She let her hand wander over his flesh, random patterns until she reached the full erection. He was thick and long. Her mouth wouldn't hold him all. But she wanted to try. She wrapped her hand around him.

He groaned and sat up meeting her in her crouched position next to his hips. He stared into her eyes for a moment then kissed her, his tongue slipping softly into her mouth and twining around hers, as if he needed her taste to survive.

Lorran fell into his kisses, addicted to the power of his mouth, to the soft manipulation of his lips. She let the world fade and savored each caress. Finally, Kei jerked back, his chest moving in long deep pants.

The same intense stare focused on her, heating her deep inside.

"Do you want to taste me?" he asked. He brushed his finger down her cheek. Lorran felt the question in the center of her stomach.

"Yes," she whispered in reply.

"Your eyes are so expressive. I can see every desire before you speak it."

"Yes." She watched him just as closely. "You always know just how to touch me, just what I want." She looked down at his thick erection. "Now, I want you in my mouth."

Kei's chest rose and fell in one long, constricted breath. He paused for a moment, as if he were gathering his strength, then reached out and took her hand in his. He guided her forward, placing her palm along the hard, warm cock. The very idea of it amazed her. She'd done this to him. She had the power to make this man hunger. Something deep inside her mind released and she smiled. She slid her fingers down his erection and felt him strain beneath her touch.

She whipped her hair over her shoulder and pushed lightly on his chest.

"Lie back," she commanded. Kei paused for a moment then slowly sank onto the bed. He was spread before her. How many times had she been in that position—her pussy open, hungry, aching for the feel of his mouth? It was his turn now. And hers.

Lorran pushed up on her hands and knees, crawling until she straddled his legs. His erection rose in front of her.

He watched her with an intensity that made her shiver. Barbaric. He looked barely human. And how close to the truth that was.

Lorran couldn't stop her slight smile. He wanted her mouth on him. But first she would indulge herself, just a little. The flood of power pushed her forward. She placed her palms on his strong thighs. The muscles were hard beneath her fingers.

She slid her hands up his thighs and beyond his hips to his flat stomach. She spread her fingers wide and lightly brushed her fingertips across his skin, absorbing his heat. Kei inhaled sharply.

She looked up and was lost for a moment in the pull of Kei's hungry gaze, but her hands never stopped. It was the control—the ability to hold himself apart—that made her want to drown him with need, have him before her pleading.

She'd learned much about Kei's desire. But he'd always been in command, always leading her to pleasure. Now, she wanted him begging for it. Instead of moving forward, she sank back on her heels.

Kei swallowed deeply as he watched the corner of her lip curl up. What in the Hells was she up to? Though she never spoke of her husband, Kei somehow knew she'd never performed this service for Brennek. Only Kei. Only he would ever feel her mouth on his cock.

A shudder of possession wracked his body as he stared at her. She was stalling. Maybe changing her mind. He curled his hands into the light sheets beneath him, fighting the sudden urge to grab her and shove his cock into her wet mouth. The strange desire to overpower her shocked him.

The creature inside him didn't seem to understand. It struggled against Kei's control—filling the human mind with erotic images of Lorran's mouth swallowing him. The almost tactile fantasy of releasing his cum down her throat. He groaned and forced the pictures away.

He opened his mouth, ready to tell her to stop. Then he looked into her eyes. She wasn't backing away.

Her smile sent tremors of masculine terror down his spine. A confident woman's smile was a threat to be heeded. She had power and now she knew it.

Her fingers lingered near the row of buttons holding the prim nightgown closed.

"Would you like me to open this?" she asked, knowing he loved to look at her breasts, had spent hours sucking on them.

He nodded. His eyes fell to her hands as she opened the buttons along her bodice. She undid the tiny catches until she reached her waist. She was bare but still hidden. And she knew it would drive him crazy.

She slipped her hands up, cupping her breasts and slowly massaged them in soft, shallow circles. She closed her eyes and let her head drop back as she moved her hands over her own skin, reaching inside the nightgown to pinch the tips of her breasts.

She could feel Kei's eyes watching her every movement. Long drugging minutes later, when her breasts ached to feel Kei's mouth, she raised her head and opened her eyes. Kei reached down and took his cock into his hand.

Lorran slapped his wrist and shook her head.

"Mine," she said.

It was the word that had filled his loving. But now, he and that deliciously large cock, belonged to her. Kei reluctantly pulled his hand back. She waited until he'd reached up above his head before she moved.

She wasn't quite sure how to proceed but Kei had taught her the power of a light touch of the tongue and long slow licks. She bent forward, hovering above his straining staff. She opened her mouth and swirled her tongue around the head of his cock. When she heard his shocked hiss, she repeated the motion before lifting her head. She couldn't stop her smile. His jaw was clenched so tightly she was sure the sounds of teeth cracking could be heard.

She took a deep breath and opened her lips taking the full thick head into her mouth. He was silky and so hard.

She relaxed and took as much of his length as she could, wanting all of him inside her. There was too much for her to take. She slid her hand around the base of his shaft, cupping the twin sacs that hung down. His hips jumped up, pushing his cock deeper into her mouth. Then finally, she pulled back and twirled her tongue around the end.

"Mine," she said again.

She bent forward and sucked his length inside, holding him deep before drawing back and flicking her tongue along the underside of the head.

Kei groaned. He'd been hard all night and now her teasing mouth was more than he could stand. The wet lick of her tongue, the steady suck of her mouth drained the blood from his head. It wasn't talent that tempted him — it was pure desire. She loved what she was doing and the power she had over him. It should have startled him, even frightened him, but he knew he was safe. In her control, he was safe.

He braced his legs and watched her pink mouth slide the length of his shaft. The dragon's voice resonated in his head as she tasted him, as she stared up and the smile of pleasure glowed in her eyes. This was the image that had allowed him to come at the waterfall that first night — the reality was way beyond the fantasy.

Her fingers gripped his thighs, tiny pinpricks of sensation as she increased the stroke of her lips, moving him deeper into her mouth.

She pulled back for a moment. He opened his mouth to growl a protest but stopped at her words. "You taste so good." Lorran licked her lips. "I love the feel of you on my tongue."

He punched his hips upward, desperate to return to the moist heat of her mouth. He couldn't seem to control his hips.

He groaned as her lips once again closed around him, sucking him deep. The sounds of her mouth pulling on his cock only made the deep aching need worse and better. And her groans. She moaned like a woman caught in her own pleasure.

The rise of his orgasm was sharp. He was coming. He thought to warn her, give her time to pull back, but the words were tangled in his mind, wrapped around the need to come in her mouth and have her take him. Moving without thought, he buried his fingers in her hair and held her. He convulsed as the climax burst on him and he released his seed into her welcoming mouth. His head fell back against the pillows.

She kept sucking, draining him. A light brush of her tongue tickled the end of his cock.

Long moments passed before his eyes uncrossed. As his breathing returned to normal, he pushed himself up on his elbows. Lorran sat between his thighs, the material from her nightgown flowing over his legs.

She smiled as she traced random patterns across his thighs. As if she sensed his observation, she looked up. And licked her lips.

Chapter 7

Kei watched Lorran as she prepared dinner. He loved watching her. It was in these quiet moments, after the lust had been satisfied, that he was able to consider the future. And was strangely content. He would die. That was the one inevitable part of his future. It gave him a certain freedom. He'd worked on his final papers, instructions to his brothers and advisors, including a nice stipend to Lorran. She didn't know about that but she deserved compensation for everything she'd done.

She'd reject the money. He knew her well enough to know that but he also knew what Riker needed to say to get Lorran to accept it. He'd written explicit instructions to his brother to promise Lorran the kingdom's support in her dragon studies if she'd accept the stipend. She would take it.

He no longer considered finding her a husband or lover to take his place. The dragon in his head refused to allow Kei to even think on it. The screams inside his mind and the gut wrenching pain the dragon created became so torturous, Kei dropped the idea. Though he felt the dragon gloating, Kei admitted in the silence of his mind that he hated the idea of another loving Lorran as he had done.

He was amazed at how well he had come to know her. He'd known her for less than two weeks and he could predict her reactions. Though there were still times when she surprised him. He knew her intimately. Not just sexually. He knew her mind.

They'd talked, in the quiet, when even the dragon's urges couldn't make his body respond. He'd told her of his own startling rise to royalty, how he'd been trained as a warrior—never expecting to inherit the kingship. His oldest brother should have succeeded their father, but he'd chosen Kei instead. He'd told her about Riker and his hopes for him as king.

She'd talked about her childhood, her marriage and the time she'd spent with dragons. She told him about her research and that of others across the land. And he could see the pity and sympathy she had for the creatures. And for their victims. She truly wanted to find a way to stop the transition.

He'd finally asked her why she'd stayed with Brennek after the change. She'd shrugged.

"It was my fault."

"What?"

"He felt like he needed to prove himself to the world. So when a dragon moved into the cliffs near our land, he decided to get rid of it himself."

"That just proves he was stupid and I don't know how his stupidity could be your fault." She'd smiled sadly and nodded. Whatever it was that had driven Brennek to fight dragons—Lorran still blamed herself.

Their own studies continued but they were no closer to slowing the dragon's appearance. After Nekane had named himself, Kei had told Lorran all the changes he'd noticed in his body and mind. She'd studiously marked them down on parchment. Whether that information would help anyone in the future, he didn't know. But if ever there was a person determined to find a way to help both the dragons and the human victims, it was Lorran.

He didn't doubt that she'd do it eventually. She was a strong woman.

Lorran rolled her shoulders back as if trying to ease some tension that had settled there. He'd offered to help with dinner but she'd smiled tiredly and told him to sit.

She was exhausted. The four days of near abstinence during her woman's time had driven him to distraction. And a desperate need to make up for the loss. For two days now, he'd done little but fuck her cunt. He didn't understand it. It wasn't like he'd gone without during those days. She'd brought him to climax with her hands. And she'd sucked him off so many times, her jaw had to ache still.

His cock rose. Hells, he thought, everything about Lorran made his cock rise these days. He was no longer appalled by the idea—more amused. The dragon was growing stronger and more vocal but its focus remained the same—fucking Lorran. As the urges became more distinct, Kei at least knew how to deal with them.

It was odd. He'd expected to be struggling frequently against the dragon, fighting the dragon's appearance on a regular basis. From what Lorran told him and what he'd read in her notes, he should be battling for control daily. But for some reason, except for occasional outbursts, the beast seemed content.

Maybe it's the sex. He considered the idea. Maybe the constant fucking was satisfying the dragon so he felt no need to rush. The only time he'd had to consciously crush the dragon was when he'd been denied access to Lorran's pussy. He'd have to suggest the idea to Lorran. Maybe they *had* found a way to stop the transition—constant fucking.

He dismissed the idea almost instantly. Lorran had said Brennek had spent his last days fucking the village women but he'd still made the change.

Kei smiled. Maybe it only worked with Lorran. He thought about a life with Lorran. They'd laugh, fight and fuck. He'd be dead from exhaustion. And Lorran would be forever pregnant. The thought stopped him. With her woman's time just passed, she wasn't pregnant but there was still a chance.

He felt the immediate urge to put his cock into her and fill her with his seed. He would have to make a provision in his final papers for any child that might issue from their time together.

"Why didn't you and Brennek have a dozen kids?" Kei asked, his voice breaking the calm silence. He thought about the way she loved to fuck and couldn't understand it. What man wouldn't be addicted to her loving?

Her back straightened and she raised her eyes, staring out the open window above the sink. The air around them vibrated with anxiety. Kei leaned forward, conscious that he'd somehow opened an old wound.

"I'm barren," she finally answered without turning around, her voice emotionless. "Brennek and I tried for children for the first five years of our marriage but nothing came of it."

"Maybe it was his problem."

She shook her head, her hair brushing across her shoulder blades. "No. His mistress bore him a child. But as his wife, I was unable to do so." Her words were soft but there was an underlying ache to them.

Pain opened up his chest. Before he had a chance to analyze the strange emotion, the beast inside him screamed. The hollow wail rejected the thought of Lorran without a child—without *his* child filling her belly. Kei's pain blended with the dragon's. He wanted to see her grow large with his seed and know that she loved the child growing inside her.

The dragon's emotions overwhelmed him, demanding a mate and offspring, to populate the world.

Kei stood. The need to move sent him to pacing the room.

Fury raged inside him—Nekane's fury—a creature who lived by instinct and didn't understand control.

"I'm going outside."

He had to get away from her. He had to put some distance between her and the dragon before the creature pounced on her again. He would walk, run, anything to burn off the energy that drove him to be inside her. To fill her.

Kei focused on walking to the door and the world beyond. Each step required all his strength. The dragon fought for control of his body. He almost sighed with relief when he reached the door.

"I understand," she whispered as the door closed behind him.

* * * * *

She stared at the closed door, amazed at how the sight caused her pain. It *was* easy to understand. She wrapped her arms around her waist, tears welling in her eyes. She'd failed another man.

All Brennek had asked from her was a child and she'd been unable to give it to him. He'd had no legitimate heir and that had driven him to prove to the world he was master of his domain. He'd ended up dying in a cave.

Now Kei, doomed to the same fate, had obviously hoped for an heir.

She took a deep breath and brushed away the tears even as they crept down her cheeks. She wouldn't cry. She'd cried too many times over her inability to conceive. She would never do so again.

At least she had the memories of Kei's loving to comfort her. She'd always remember the feel of Kei moving in her body, the lovely glide of his shaft between her legs and the heat of his mouth on her skin, on her sex. Her body began to ache at the thought.

She pushed it aside. It wouldn't do to dwell on it. If nothing else, life had taught her to accept what she couldn't change. She made a quick dinner and ate it silently. Who knew when Kei would return? She left a plate warming in the oven and finally went to bed.

She curled onto her side and stared at the dying fire. She'd grown used to Kei's body next to hers. She'd have to re-learn to sleep without his weight in her bed. And without his loving each night to exhaust her.

She used the memories to relax her body. She wanted him. Again. Always. She slid her hand under the blankets and began to lightly touch herself, imagining it was Kei's hand. The soft caresses allowed her to drift into a light doze. Heat and fire waited for her in sleep.

He pulled back the blankets and spread her legs.

"Let me inside you, let me fill you," he whispered.

"Yes, come to me."

He climbed on the bed and shoved his cock inside her with no prelude. She was wet and open for him.

He groaned as he drove deep. "You feel so good," he whispered. "Your cunt clings to me, like you never want to let me go."

I don't. She kept the words silent as she always did.

"Mine."

"Yes."

Kei watched her twist under the blankets. He'd walked to the waterfall, trying to work through the anger. At his own loss and at Lorran's. It was insane of course. He'd never expected to get a child on Lorran. The idea hadn't come to him until that night but once the thought was there, it had been impossible to shake.

Eventually, he'd climbed the mountain to Effron's lair. Effron had ignored him on this visit.

Kei was again stunned by the steady waves of loneliness and despair that emanated from the dragon. It was easy to see how those emotions quickly turned to rage—rage against a world that didn't understand.

Nekane had screamed for Lorran and had dragged Kei away, as if seeing the other dragon's empty life was too much for the beast. The awareness that Lorran would be able to fill the hollow space in his chest seeped into his thoughts. Where before, he'd turned from her, desperate to prove to himself and the dragon that he would stand alone—this time he accepted his need for her.

He'd returned to the cabin. And found her like this. She was dreaming. Her body warm with musk. She was lusting.

His cock leapt at the sweet smell of her wet cunt. She was waiting to be filled. He ripped off the blankets. Her beautiful breasts were cupped in her own hands, her nipples tight between her fingers. She rocked her hips upward as if fucking some imaginary lover. He moved quickly. He had to fulfill the crying need of her body.

She woke up as his hands touched the insides of her thighs. He stared at her wet sex, spread wide before him.

"Mine," he whispered, mirroring the voice in his head. He bent down and kissed the very tip of her pretty little cunt. Then, slowly licked downward, needing a hint of her taste to linger on his tongue.

"But, Kei, I thought—"

He didn't know what she was going to say but her words transformed into a gasp and then a moan as he sucked slowly on her clit. She was so wet. He slurped up all her pussy juice and licked her until more flowed from her. Her cries turned to pleas. He feasted long on her sex, sating himself and binding her to him with pleasure. He didn't rush. Instead, he spent time loving her, arousing her, giving back to her all the pleasure she gave to him. The dragon rumbled contentedly inside his head.

Then, the images that had haunted him—her ripe with his child—burst into his head. He pulled back. He needed to give her his seed and wanted to feel her accept it. The urge drove him upward. He moved up her body and slid his cock into her sex in one fluid glide.

He groaned as her wet cunt sucked his cock inside. He was beyond thought, beyond rational behavior. He needed to come inside her, to fill her with his seed. He had no control, no restraint. He thrust inside her twice, then again, feeling the steady rise of a sharp clear orgasm.

He shoved in deep and his world released. He flooded her with his cum.

Seconds later, the strength sapped from his body, he collapsed on top of her. He didn't have the energy to move off and in this position, his cock stayed buried in her cunt. He was going to need more of her pussy in a while so he wanted to stay inside.

Lorran shifted underneath him and he raised his head. Her eyes were clouded with pain and he had the sudden urge to nuzzle her. He rubbed his nose along her cheek, soothing her.

"I can't provide you an heir, Kei," she said after a moment.

He leaned back and stared at her in amazement. "Is that what you thought?" She shrugged but he saw through the casual movement. This was the source of the pain. "It never occurred to me until three hours ago that you might get pregnant. I wasn't fucking you for an heir. I was fucking you because I can't seem to stop."

She smiled and he felt her relax underneath him. "I've noticed."

"I don't *want* to stop," he said, knowing it was an important distinction.

He pushed himself up on his elbows and rubbed his softening cock inside her passage. The light friction immediately returned him to a hard state. Lorran gasped as he pulsed deep inside her. He knew she liked this, liked the short massaging pulses far inside her pussy.

"I want to move inside this tight cunt until you ache from need," Kei growled. Lorran gasped. "And then I'll give you what you ask for."

He kept whispering to her as he rocked inside her, filling her mind with his voice as he filled her body with his cock. Her eyes grew vague as she lost herself once more.

This was what he wanted her to remember when he was gone. He clamped down on his own need to thrust hard and worked for her, pleasuring her body with his hands, mouth and cock until the sun began to creep up in the sky. Then, her mind lost to all but him, he sank one final time into her cunt and once again filled her pussy with his seed.

* * * * *

Kei grimaced as he washed in the miniscule tub. His knees were up against his chest and his shoulders were wider than the edge of the small tub. But it was a quick way to get clean. Maybe later he could convince Lorran to go to the waterfall—enjoy the pleasures of the warm pond. The hazy visions that seemed to characterize the dragon's thoughts instantly formed pictures of Kei and Lorran, naked on the rocks beside the waterfall. She'd watched him that first night. Now he could enjoy her fully—her lips on his cock, his mouth drinking from her cunt. The dragon grumbled his agreement.

He'd give her the day to rest. Nekane's protest was a soft growl. Kei shook his head. It was strange how he'd adapted to the dragon's voice. He almost expected reactions from the beast.

The low tones of a man's voice outside the cabin drew Kei from his thoughts. He stood and draped a towel around his waist. It was odd to hear another human.

The only contact with the world beyond the cabin had been Kei's messages to the Castle.

No one visited Lorran. The town didn't approve of her. She'd told him people had threatened her when she'd first moved in. Now, most ignored her.

Flicking his damp hair over his shoulder, Kei walked to the window and looked out.

A tall burly man with an open friendly face and ready smile stood listening intently as Lorran spoke. The male reached out and patted her softly on her shoulder. Then he spoke and Lorran smiled. Kei couldn't hear the man's words. A violent roar in his head blocked the sound.

Kei felt the muscles in the back of his neck begin to twist. He stared down at his hand, watching it tighten and curl until it formed a claw.

Lorran's gentle laughter floated across the clear air. She nodded and watched the man walk back toward town. Seconds later, she came back inside.

"That was Mr. Fiya from the General Store. He was delivering—" She stopped and looked at him. "What's wrong?"

"I can smell him on you." Kei didn't recognize his own voice. The sound was deep and low, like an animal's growl. "He touched you." He lifted his head and stared at her. The dark haze he associated with the dragon didn't block his vision. It intensified it. Everything about her was clear. Every strand of hair was separated and every scent catalogued. Every breath she took was gathered in his lungs. Kei blinked and tried to push the fog away.

It was happening. The beast was battling for control. A male had touched his mate! He turned his neck, stretching it up and twisting around, fighting for final domination over the body. "He touched you," he heard himself repeat.

As he said the words, he stepped forward—the human struggled to deny each footstep, but the dragon was too strong.

Mine. Take mine! Beyond the words, Kei felt the dragon's fierce need to possess Lorran. Kei resisted, calling on every strength he had. And still he walked forward.

"He just touched my shoulder." Lorran shook her head. And stepped back.

It burst into his mind—backing away, running from him.

Leave? No! Mine!

Kei knew that Lorran had heard the dragon's mental cry when she shook her head and took another step back. Kei watched the movement and the dragon screamed. The bellow reverberated through the small cabin. Lorran slapped her hands over her ears to block the horrifying noise.

Kei felt his awareness fading, losing even the ability to fight the beast.

She inched away. The movement felt familiar. It took a moment for her to remember—this was just like her dream. She was being hunted by a dragon. Stalked by the man she loved.

All semblance of humanity was gone from the black eyes that stared at her. But it was more than just the black eyes that warned her Kei was no longer in charge. Waves of rage emanated from his body. The dragon had taken control of the human mind and was close to freeing itself from the physical human constraints. When the creature appeared, the house wouldn't be able to contain it. It would turn on her. That long contained fury would explode.

Unwilling to look away, she stepped backward, and placed her foot on the hem of her gown. She went down with a thud. Kei still moved forward.

Lorran scrambled back on her hands and feet, trying to escape. Her heart pumped blood erratically through her veins.

"Kei, please," she said when she could gather enough air to speak.

Mine! The word entered her mind but Kei did not speak it.

"No." She shook her head.

Mine! The creature repeated.

"No, please."

He bent down and began to crawl the last few feet to her. The rough wool of her gown flipped upward, baring her legs to her thighs. She moved to pull the material down but he was there—his hands reaching for her, grabbing her thighs and pulling her toward him.

"Kei, please. Don't let him win." She called to the human inside—hoping he was still there, still able to react.

He stared down at her spread legs. His hands tightened on her knees.

"Please, Kei, don't do this."

The fear in her voice reached deep inside him. It shocked him, sending strength to his body. He threw himself back, lunging for the door. He had to get away— had to get free. He ripped the door open and stumbled onto the wooden porch. He took a deep breath, trying to clear Lorran's scent from his nostrils. The smell of her fear still haunted his senses. He stalked off the porch and paced the yard.

Male scent on mine!

Nekane's scream throbbed in Kei's skull, making it almost impossible to think. The only choice was to move.

He took off in a run, away from Lorran, into the woods. He raced down the narrow trail toward town. The smell of the man who'd touched Lorran was easily traced and he started to follow it.

The gut-tearing rage boiled inside again. *Kill male.*

Kei jerked himself to a stop, gripping a small tree to keep himself from moving forward, from hunting the man who'd dared touch his woman!

He forced himself to take long slow breaths, to cleanse his body of everything but the smell of the soil and the trees lining the path. Fog blurred his thoughts but Kei refused to release his hold on the tree. It was the only thing binding him to the earth.

Time slowly returned to focus and Kei looked up. The sun was almost set. He'd been gone for hours. He looked around and sniffed the air, hating the animal-like movement but needing the dragon's senses. The scent of the shopkeeper had faded and there was no smell of blood. Kei looked down at his hands. They were clean except for the tree sap. So he hadn't killed the man.

Nekane grumbled in response. The beast wasn't happy. Kei could sense the dragon's future plan. When Nekane was finally released from the constraints of the human body, he would return and kill the shopkeeper.

Lorran had told him at the beginning that it was unsafe for him to return home because he would hurt the people around him. Now he knew why. The dragon held the memory and the rage. It would return to punish any that offended it.

But Kei was back in control—for now. Triumph pulsed through his veins giving him strength.

And another erection.

Lorran. He wanted her. Wanted to fuck her, drive his tongue into her pussy. Claim her so she'd never think of another man.

Yes. Yes. More. Mine.

But he wouldn't. Kei crushed the dragon's rebellion. The creature howled inside his head once again.

Barely holding onto the last bit of humanity, Kei started to plan. It was time. He had to leave.

Lorran sat by the fire, ostensibly reading but Kei knew she'd been staring blankly at the pages. She looked up when he entered and fear flickered in her eyes. She quickly hid it but it was too late. He knew it was there. He braced himself for the dragon's cry. The beast growled softly, but remained steady.

"I'm leaving."

"What? Now? It's dark outside."

"It's best. I have to leave. Now."

She set the book aside and stood, moving swiftly toward him. Kei backed away. "Don't come near me."

"You won't hurt me, Kei. I know that."

He nodded. "I won't, but what about him?" He tapped the side of his head. "I can't control him much longer. It's finally happening." He'd wondered why the dragon had stayed silent for so long—now, it seemed the beast was ready to appear. "I have to go home. Deliver my papers and speak to my brothers before the final change."

"But—"

"Lorran, don't. You did your best. I hope anything you learned from me will help others."

"Let me come with you."

"Don't." He found the courage to look at her. "I won't have you sacrificing yourself the way you did with Cronan. This creature inside me would destroy you."

"I don't see it as a sacrifice."

He felt her words in his chest. He could have her. She would come with him and stay by his side.

"I know what's going to happen to me. Living with that horror will be bad enough. Taking *you* to that level of the Hells would drive me insane."

He waited, watching her until she nodded, until he was sure she understood. If she cared about him, she had to let him go. He couldn't bear the thought of her living in the dark corner of a cave. Only the Gods knew what the dragon would to do her.

He had to go.

He looked around the room. He had nothing to take. Nothing here belonged to him.

Except her.

Mine.

He ignored the voice, using the strength embedded in him since childhood. He could walk through fire, endure unimaginable pain—he could walk away from her.

He stopped at the door knowing he had to say something. "Thank you. For everything." Lorran followed, staying just out of touching range. Tears pooled along the lower edge of her eyes making them glitter in the pale candlelight. "You're an amazing woman."

And he stepped into the dark night, the dragon screaming in his head.

No!

* * * * *

No!

Nekane's wail echoed through the empty room. She watched the door close behind him and felt her own heart cry in response. Sympathy for the dragon—and for the man destined for death. Tears poured unnoticed down her cheeks. She wanted to race after him, to drag him back, plead with him to stay but to what end?

The dragon was rising in him.

And Kei knew it.

He was leaving to protect her.

"Dammit."

She could go after him but he didn't want that. His honor, which was one of the many things she'd learned about him, wouldn't let him stay. He was afraid Nekane would take over. Those shocking few moments this afternoon when the dragon had stalked her across the room frightened her. She shivered at the memory. Kei had completely disappeared.

She'd been afraid, truly afraid of the beast inside him. *Mine.*

Kei had said it to her often but it was only when the dragon had screamed it did she understand its true meaning. He wanted her to belong to him, completely. He wanted to consume her.

Lorran sank to the floor and stared blankly at the fire. The room was deathly quiet. How was she going to do it? How was she going to learn to live without him?

Her worst fears had come true. She'd fallen in love with him.

Chapter 8

"Well, well, well. He's back."

Kei ignored Kafe's mocking greeting. Nekane growled quietly in Kei's head. The dragon either sensed Kei's feelings toward his brother or he was a good judge of character. Kei had been back for a full day but this was Kafe's first appearance.

"You'll need to see that the North Shore Treaty is finalized." Kei held up the document to Riker.

The young man nodded. Kei watched his brother for a moment. Some people would think he was too young to rule but Kei knew Riker's strength. Like Kei, Riker had trained as a warrior. Now, he would be king.

Kei glanced down at the paper in his hand. He had always imagined he'd have a son to teach, a son to raise and train as his successor. He'd never thought that he'd have hours instead of years to pass along the important information. But Riker was smart and honest. Unfortunately, the same couldn't be said about Kafe. Kafe was clever but devious. And ten minutes older than Kei.

"What? No greeting for me? Really Kei, how rude." Kafe brushed the tips of his fingernails across the velvet vest he wore. "Or is there something more appropriate to call you now? Dragon-spawn perhaps?"

Kei looked up at the mirror image of himself. The mystical connection between twins was rubbish, as far as Kei was concerned. He didn't feel connected at all to Kafe, except for a mutual dislike. Naturally, Riker had told Kafe about the dragon attack. Riker didn't understand the depth of Kafe's hatred for Kei.

Kei had done his best to shield his younger brother from Kafe's true nature. Now that Riker would be king, he would have to be warned. He had to know that Kafe couldn't be trusted.

"Kafe, what do you want?" Kei asked doing his best to sound bored. It would irritate Kafe and maybe he'd leave.

"Just what's mine by right."

Kei knew Kafe meant the kingdom. He'd always believed *he* should have been chosen to lead. Their father had decided differently.

"The kingdom will go to my heir."

"Well, unless you've implanted a seed in the past three weeks, that looks like it will be me." Kafe's eyes hardened. "You haven't gotten some bitch pregnant, have you? What's the name of the whore who nursed your pitiful life back to health?"

Kei didn't remember moving. He was over the table and his hands wrapped around Kafe's throat before the final words of the sentence were said.

His fingers dug into the skin as he squeezed the life out of the offender's throat. *Kill him. Kill.*

"Kei, stop. What are you doing?"

Kei snapped back to himself as Riker grabbed his wrists and tried to pull him away. "Let him go."

Fighting Nekane every inch, Kei forced his hands to unclench. His twin dropped to the floor, gasping for air, red streaks appearing on his throat.

Kafe glared up at his brother. "You attack me over a woman? She must be quite a good—" he paused. Kei pulled his fist back, ready to break Riker's hold if Kafe said one disrespectful word against Lorran. The dragon grumbled in agreement.

"Nurse," Kafe finally finished. He stood and brushed off his leathers with delicate fingers. "I didn't know she meant so much to you." The gleam that shone in his eyes worried Kei for a moment but he let it go. In a few days, none of this would matter.

"I don't want you thinking about her at all."

Kafe shrugged then winced. Kei felt a momentary regret. He'd hurt his brother. Kafe's neck was already bruising. But he had deserved it, that and more.

Like an animal pacing a cage, Nekane hovered just beyond the physical world. Kei took a deep breath. It was getting harder and harder to keep him under control. It would be a day, maybe two before the creature overtook him completely. The dragon growled his displeasure. *Kill him. Kill.*

The dragon screamed in his head, once again calling for Lorran. *Get mine!*

Kei barely heard, and didn't acknowledge, Kafe's farewell. It was difficult to focus around the dragon's cries.

He waited until Kafe was gone before turning to Riker. He was young to be crowned but Kei knew his brother was smart, brave and he had a conscience. He'd do well.

"The first thing you have to do when I die is banish Kafe."

Riker's eyes widened. "What?"

"He'll cause problems. Father asked me to let him stay. I won't make the same mistake with you. Outlaw him. I can't. You have to." Kei shrugged, looking more casual than he felt. "He's got money so he'll hire men. You'll have the loyalty of the guard here. Use that."

Riker nodded. There was a flicker of guilt in his brother's eyes. That was good. He was already thinking about getting rid of Kafe. It was something Kei should have done a year ago, but he'd made a promise. Riker would have to address it. There was so much he had to leave for Riker.

Including Lorran. His instructions in his papers were explicit. He trusted Riker to follow through.

Kei cleared his throat.

"Right. Now, the North Shore can be held. The rebellion was more of a peasants' protest. Send someone..."

* * * * *

Lorran stepped out on the porch and let the morning sun hit her eyes. She'd spent all of yesterday and the day before inside the cabin—sobbing. Her eyes were red and puffy from the two day crying jag. With a quiet sniff, she pushed her shoulders back. She wouldn't cry for him any longer. He was gone. Of his own choice.

But the truth showed itself even as she tried to deny it. Kei had left to protect her. Nekane was growing stronger. Kei was losing control. She paced the wood porch. She would go to town for some supplies. It would be a good excuse to hear the latest gossip. It was going to be on everyone's lips when the king turned into a dragon.

A cold breeze sent a shiver across her arms. It was early. The sun hadn't had time to warm the earth. She'd wait until mid-day and then go. Long enough to hear what they were saying.

A boot scuffing the wood platform drew her attention. She spun around and her heart stopped.

"Kei!" She ran the four steps to him. As she threw her arms around his neck, she realized something was wrong. She jerked back and stepped away. "You're not Kei."

It was Kei's mirror image. But the soft edges of his face and the cruel glow in his eyes were so dramatically different from Kei's she was surprised she'd mistaken him for even a moment.

"Who are you?" She had a vague recollection of stories about twin princes but she'd ignored the tales. She'd turned her back on that life five years ago when she'd chosen to study dragons instead of returning to her father's house.

"I'm Kafe. Kei's brother, as you see. Kei didn't mention me? How unlike him. He usually can't say enough about me." The smarmy grin made Lorran's jaw ache. She took another step away. "Kei sent me. He was worried about you, worried that you're out here unprotected." Lorran inched back. He followed her across the porch. "He needs you. He hated to admit it but he wants you with him."

She had to suppress the ache his words created. She didn't trust him. Kei had left to protect her. Why would he call her to him?

"I don't believe you."

"It's true. He misses you."

Her stomach clenched. Oh, how she wanted that to be true, but Kei wouldn't call her.

"I think you'd better leave."

"Not without you." The charming smile disappeared and a jubilant meanness was reflected in his eyes. "You can appear before your beloved Kei covered in bruises, or not. The choice is up to you." He paused. "On second thought—" He swung his hand out and slapped her hard against the face. Lorran fell to the ground, her cheek burning. "A few bruises wouldn't be such a bad idea," Kafe said. "Now, I can stop there, or I can beat you bloody. Either will suit my purposes."

Lorran didn't respond. Her head vibrated from the vicious blow. She barely noticed when he dragged her to her feet and pushed her toward another soldier. The warrior caught her against his chest then quickly tied her hands together with a rope.

Kafe gripped her chin in his fingers and lifted her head, inspecting her face. "Yes, that should bruise nicely, but give me any trouble and I'll present you to Kei as a crumpled pile of human flesh." She glared silently at him. Kafe smiled. "Yes, it's almost impossible to believe we're brothers, isn't it?"

* * * * *

Kei stalked in front of the fireplace, turned around and repeated the path. Energy raged through his body. A dragon's energy.

The damned beast wouldn't let him rest.
Mine.

The petulant voice echoed through Kei's head.

Mine! The dragon insisted.

163

It wanted Lorran. Kei curled his hands into fists, squeezing until his knuckles turned white. He had to fight it—had to fight the urge to send for Lorran. If he sent an express, she could be here by mid-morning. She would come if he summoned her. She was loyal and too damn caring.

Yes. Mine.

"No!" Kei pounded his fist against the stone mantel. Pain shot up his arm but he barely recognized it. The rock cracked underneath the weight of his hand. The dragon's strength was entering his human body, just like the voice was always in his head now.

"Your M-Majesty?"

Kei straightened and turned to face the maid. He recognized her. She'd shared his bed on a few occasions. She swallowed convulsively and stared at him with wide eyes.

This is what I've become. A beast that my own servants fear.

The young woman walked cautiously toward him. She was beautiful, tall and sleek, with full breasts that would fit perfectly in his hands. Her gown was low cut, revealing a deep cleavage. She'd been an eager bedmate. Now she was frightened of him.

He took a deep breath and inhaled her scent. He paused and waited for the dragon's growl—waited for lust to slam into his body.

Nothing. She was a beautiful woman and he felt no desire to fuck her. The dragon didn't seem to even notice her presence in the room.

"What is it?"

"I was asked to deliver this to you."

Kei silently took the note from her shaking hand. Kafe's recognizable scrawl made the muscles along Kei's back tighten to the point of snapping.

"Thank you." He dismissed her, barely noticing as she left, and stared at the note.

Meet me at Turphen's Rock. I have something you want.

It wasn't signed but that didn't surprise Kei. Kafe would want to disclaim knowledge later. What was his brother up to now? An ambush?

It didn't matter. The papers were signed and logged. Riker was his heir. And Kafe knew that Kei would be dead within days anyway.

Kei moved quickly, gathering his sword and battle leathers. He didn't know Kafe's plan but he'd learned long ago not to discount him.

Turphen's Rock had been their meeting spot as children. It was just a short walk away but far enough so prying eyes from the Castle couldn't see them practicing with wooden swords and hitting each other with sticks.

Kei stormed through the forest without trying to conceal his progress. He walked into the clearing beside the huge rock and waited. The dragon's senses were tuned to the forest around them. Kei let the awareness flow into him and instantly he could see beyond the clearing, picking up minute details about the men hidden in the forest.

So it *was* to be an ambush. It was almost easier this way, Kei decided. He would die here, as a man. Instead of backed into a cave and hunted as a dragon.

Mine.

Kei ignored the dragon's plea. The creature's cries for Lorran were becoming a consistent part of his life.

"Kafe, what do you want?" Kei called out.

Kafe stepped out of the shadows but stayed at the edge of the clearing. "Oh, it's not what I want. It's what you want."

"Kafe, I don't have time for this. You've got men surrounding the clearing." If he'd wanted to, he could have told Kafe where each one was hiding, but he decided to just get this over. "You're planning on killing me, that's fine, but can you do it without the dramatics?" Kei unsheathed his sword and prepared for the attack. He couldn't go down without a fight. It went against his nature. "Riker becomes king no matter how I die, and we both know that day isn't far away. I'm actually pleased you took the initiative to do this."

The irritation on Kafe's face was worth every mocking word. But then, the smugness returned. "Oh, I still have a chance to be king. Particularly when you're outlawed. It shouldn't be difficult to have your last will voided. You were a man under the influence of a dragon."

Kei held himself still, not letting any fear show. Riker was smart. He would be able to handle it.

"But, since you're going to sign over the kingship to me, we'll save all the hassles of a bloody civil war."

Kafe's confidence was worrisome.

"Why would I sign anything over to you?" Kei asked.

Kafe swung his head in silent command to someone behind him. A warrior walked forward. Dragging Lorran.

"Mine!" Nekane screamed the word. It echoed off the trees and disappeared into the night.

Kafe pulled back and then stared at his brother. "Was that the beast? It has a voice. And it really wants this little lady here." Kafe grabbed Lorran by the upper arm and pulled her forward. Her hands were tied in front of her and she stumbled, falling against Kafe's chest.

Nekane growled.

Kei took a deep breath and stared at Lorran, ignoring his brother and the re-positioning of men in the forest.

"Did he hurt you?"

Lorran lifted her eyes and shook her head. A gag blocked her words. A dark purple bruise marred the delicate skin of her cheek. Nekane screamed again.

"She's fine," Kafe said. "Oh, you mean, did I rape her? Not yet. But I suppose I'll get around to it. Though, I'm not sure I can get it up for a dragon whore."

Kei tensed. He was trained to think during the chaos of war, but Nekane's howls filled his head, blocking the ability to plan. Kei raised his sword and started forward.

A knife glittered in Kafe's hand. "I wouldn't do that. I'll kill her right now. Give me the kingdom and I'll let you have her. And when you're dead, I'll protect her. If not, I'll give her over to my men to be used at will."

"No!"

Kei's mind turned black. In a blinding moment before all thought faded, he felt his body explode.

It was done.

* * * * *

Lorran screamed around the tight gag as the dragon materialized in the small clearing. One moment Kei stood before them, and the next, he was gone. Nekane bellowed as he opened his wings. He was huge, dominating the open space with his long body and powerful tail. His wings brushed the trees. The green and purple scales shimmered in the dark light. His huge head swung forward, the black eyes searching for Lorran.

"Kill the dragon," Kafe commanded as he took a step back. The forest erupted. Men poured from behind the trees and climbed over rocks. Swords glinted in the moonlight and the whiz of arrows filled the night sky.

Kafe pushed Lorran toward a soldier. "Keep her. I want to see this." He folded his arms over his chest and watched as his men began to beat on the dragon.

Lorran struggled in the warrior's grip. He squeezed her wrists in his strong hands, the pressure growing as his eyes widened. Nekane was moving closer. The swords hacking at his skin had little effect. Arrows bounced off his tough hide as nothing more than minor irritations. But there were so many of them—too many men fighting the enraged dragon.

A wall of men attacked his side. Nekane turned and opened his mouth. Flames blasted across the night sky followed by the wails of pain. But more men followed, approaching him from behind. The creature twisted, trying to shake off the soldiers.

Nekane's screams of fury turned to pain as a sword bit through his tough hide. He swung his tail—knocking the attacker into the brush.

Lorran twisted her head to the side, pulling and sliding the gag down. She had to get to Nekane. Had to get him away. They were killing him. She felt the strap give. She spat out the cloth they'd shoved in her mouth.

"Nekane, no! Go. Get away."

"So, the beast has a name," Kafe mocked. "No matter what you call it. It's a dragon. Kill it," he ordered again.

The man holding Lorran pulled her backwards, drawing Nekane deeper into the mass of warriors and archers. Tracks of blood began to drip down the dragon's hide. One brave soldier raced forward and crammed an arrow into an open sword wound.

Nekane's scream echoed through the trees. An arrow pierced his neck. He stretched his neck up and bellowed. Fire burst from deep inside his throat.

"No!" Lorran fought to get to him. Tears flowed down her cheeks and clogged her throat. They were killing him. "Leave him alone."

"Mine!?"

The word was clear and distinct above the crack of swords against the solid dragon hide. Pain and confusion rang through Nekane's voice as if he didn't understand what was happening. Another warrior broke through, slicing into Nekane's front leg.

The dragon reared back, his massive wings flapping, knocking over men and swaying trees.

"Don't back off. After it. Kill the creature."

Men continued to attack with swords followed by knives. The dragon roared. Lorran gasped as the sound penetrated deep into her mind.

Nekane tensed, crouching low, then jumping. His massive legs threw him into the air and the powerful wings lifted him. Arrows chased as he escaped. Lorran watched, praying for his safety as he turned and flew out of sight.

"The dragon is vanquished!" Kafe raised his clean sword in victory. "We will celebrate. Lay out the feast. We have banished the dragon."

"We?" Lorran tore free from her captor and rammed her bound hands into Kafe's chest. The large man rocked back on his heels. "You didn't do anything except set him up, you weasel. He's your brother."

Hatred reigned in Kafe's eyes. "He's a beast and if you want to be known as anything more than a dragon's whore, you'll watch what you say." Kafe put his knife back in its scabbard. "I might have use for you in my household. My brother seemed to enjoy your talents. I'm interested to find out what you did to him that was so special. You must be one incredible fuck."

Days of no sleep and the pain of watching Kei's final change had thinned the line of Lorran's control. Without thinking, she swung her tied hands. Her knuckles connected with Kafe's mouth. Blood splattered as his lip split.

"You bitch! Guards, take her. She's attacked the crown prince."

Hands immediately landed on her arms and shoulders. Lorran didn't struggle. Her hand throbbed but she was satisfied. Kafe would bear her mark.

"Take her to the dungeon. Don't hurt her. I want her clean and begging me for release."

"I'll die first."

"That's always an option, yes."

* * * * *

Lorran sat on the edge of the filthy cot. She'd been here for two days. At least, that was how she calculated it based on the meager meals they brought her.

She was unharmed, just alone in the almost complete darkness of the cell. No one had touched her or even spoken to her.

Nekane was out there. Somewhere.

Alone.

The memory of that day had kept her awake. The poor creature hadn't understood what was happening. He'd only wanted to protect Lorran—to get to the woman he considered his...his mate.

Her heart stuttered.

Could that be it? She'd seen a dragon's strength—and the rage and anger that permeated the creatures. Then she remembered Nekane calming, relaxing when she touched Kei.

It suddenly became clear. Nekane stayed calm, let Kei take the lead, as long as Lorran was near. And safe. She shuddered. She could still hear Nekane's screams as he tried to get to her. To protect her.

She stood and began to pace the room. She quickly went through Nekane's appearances. He'd made himself known three times—when he'd been denied access to Lorran's sex, when another man had touched her, and when she was threatened.

Everyone assumed dragons were indiscriminate in their search for sex. Nekane hadn't been interested in the woman Lorran had brought from town. What if the dragon was searching for much more than just a fucking partner? What if he was looking for a mate? And all the women were merely candidates until he found the right one?

Could that be it?

Nekane was an oversexed, jealous, protective creature who had claimed her as his own. If she could convince him she was safe, wouldn't leave him and wanted him, was it possible he would retreat and let Kei return?

She sagged against the back wall. "And how am I supposed to convince a dragon of all that?"

She looked around the cell. The first thing was getting out of the dungeon. She had to get to Nekane.

Light entered the room in a streak across the floor. It took Lorran a minute to realize the door had been opened and bright lanterns carried in. She blinked and pulled back from the light.

Instead of the guards she'd expected, three matrons walked in.

"Good morning, mistress. We've come to help you with your bath." The woman's tone was courteous and humble. A far cry from the growls of the guards as they brought her meals.

"What's happening?"

"The crown prince, soon to be His Majesty, asked us to assist you with your bath and take you to him."

Lorran felt her cheeks pull up in a facsimile of a smile. Kafe had obviously discovered who her parents were. No one had informed him that she'd been disowned when she'd taken up the study of dragons.

As much as she would have liked to disobey Kafe, she had a better chance of helping Nekane if she were out of the dungeon.

Lorran followed the women out of the cell, silently thanking the Goddesses who were obviously watching out for her. She could only hope the Gods were doing the same for Kei.

Lorran hurried through the bath. After dressing in a fine silk gown with thin straps that left her shoulders bare, Lorran was led to a large door. Her escort bowed before turning and walking away.

This should be interesting, she thought as she walked into the Great Hall.

Kafe waited at the far end, talking with an older couple. Lorran tensed as soon as she saw them.

Her parents.

Her steps slowed as she reached the end of the room. She hadn't seen her parents in years. They hadn't changed much.

"Ah, there she is," Kafe greeted with a smile. He held out his hand to her. "Did you have a nice rest?" He said the words distinctly, obviously warning her to keep quiet about the fact that she'd spent the last two days in a dungeon.

"It was fine. I'm rested enough to go home." If he didn't want her parents to know she'd been locked up, perhaps she could use that to her advantage. She needed to get to Nekane. The beginnings of a plan were forming.

"Nonsense, my dear, your parents are here. To celebrate our nuptials."

Laughter broke from Lorran's mouth. She recovered enough to stare at him. "Are you insane?"

"Daughter, that is no way to speak to a king." Her father's correcting voice brought back years of memories — sitting properly, listening to his lectures on the appropriate behavior of a princess. "I've given my approval for the marriage. You will be wed."

"Hello, Father. Mother. I'm sorry you came all this way for nothing." She looked at her parents. "I'm a widow, Father. There will be no wedding between Kafe and myself. I'd rather die. And Father, he's not a king. His brother is king."

"Not for long." Kafe folded his arms over his chest and smiled tightly at Lorran. "The Kings' Council is on its way. As soon as they arrive, Kei and that beast he's become will be declared outlaws, and everything he's done will be undone. I'll be listed as my father's heir."

"Lorran, this is a good match. You'll be a queen." Her mother's soft voice evoked a new set of emotions. She'd seen her mother subservient to her father all their lives. It was expected. Lorran had modeled herself after her mother during her own marriage. But she'd learned strength and independence after her husband had been transformed into a dragon.

"Where's Riker?" she asked Kafe, ignoring her mother's pleading. Kei had trusted his younger brother. Lorran needed to talk with him.

"He's not here."

"Where is he?" she asked again.

"Gone." He paused and she saw again that excited cruelty in his eyes. "Dragon slaying."

She suddenly found it hard to breathe. Of course. Riker had gone to kill Nekane. It was what Kei would have wanted.

"You bastard."

"Me?" Kafe opened his eyes wide and looked at her with excessive innocence. "I'm not the one climbing a mountain to kill my brother."

"You're stealing his kingdom instead."

Kafe's face turned hard—all trace of mockery or teasing gone. "I don't have to steal what should have been mine in the first place. It will be over when the Kings' Council arrives in two days."

"Well, until that happens, I think I'll stay in my room."

Lorran turned and walked away.

"She'll come around," her father said confidently.

"She'll have to," Kafe added.

Lorran stepped into the hallway and her confidence melted away. She didn't have much time. Kafe was right. As soon as the Kings' Council arrived and declared Kei an outlaw, everything would revert to Kafe. Riker would be banished and she'd have to marry Kafe.

Despite her strong words, marriage to Kafe was a definite possibility. It wouldn't take much. She wouldn't even have to agree to it. Kafe could simply declare her his wife by King's Right.

She kept moving, walking until she found the garden. Just beyond the wall, the forest stretched for miles. Where had Nekane gone? His escape would have been tracked. A wounded, screaming dragon wouldn't have passed unnoticed.

If Riker had gone there to kill Nekane, surely she could find it.

She had to try. To see if they could do the impossible and have a dragon release his hold.

Chapter 9

Finding a dragon proved ridiculously simple. Villagers had traced Nekane's progress. They looked at her with suspicion and then issued dire warnings about the appetites of dragons.

"I'll be fine," she responded, following their directions and ignoring their advice. The afternoon sun was harsh as she finished the climb up the mountain. Nekane had chosen a cave nearby. She'd told Kei that dragons were dangerous to their home territories. This dragon was obviously no different.

She just hoped she was in time. Riker's horse waited in a small clearing about twenty feet from the cave opening.

"Riker?"

"Lorran!" Riker spun around, his battle leathers half on. "What are you doing here?"

"Riker, you can't do this." She didn't realize how close she was to tears until she saw him preparing to kill Nekane.

"Lorran, go back. You don't want to be here for this." She didn't move. "Kei wouldn't want you here."

She saw the sadness in his eyes and had to speak. "He's your brother."

"He's a dragon." Riker's voice was cold and hard. She knew that Kei had taught him that—taught him to separate his emotions, to crush them when a job needed to be done.

"I can bring him back."

Riker paused for a moment then shook his head, as if afraid to believe in her words. "No one's been able to reverse the process. Not once the transition is complete." The resignation in his voice pulled the strength from Lorran's body. What if she was wrong? What if Kei was gone forever? "And let me tell you, that's a full grown dragon in there."

Lorran looked toward the cave. Kei was in there, locked inside a furious dragon. And she had to get him out. Or she had to try.

"Riker—"

"I spent hours today, calling to Kei, trying to get him back. There is no way he can beat the dragon."

She shook her head. "No, he can't."

"Then I have to do this." He placed his hand on the hilt of his sword. He looked so young, so brave. And so unhappy. He knew what he was doing—killing his own brother—but he also knew he had no choice. "Kei wouldn't want to live like that."

Lorran had to struggle not to agree. Riker was right. Kei would rather die than spend his life in a dragon's form, but if she could bring him back...

"Let me try."

"Haven't you been listening to me?" Riker took her shoulders in his hands and gave her a quick frustrated shake, tension finally cracking the stoic face.

"Yes. Kei can't defeat the dragon. No human can. But what if the dragon retreats?"

"How?"

Lorran shook her head. She couldn't tell him she planned to seduce a dragon. "Give me one day. What can it hurt?"

"You. That beast will kill you."

"Nekane won't hurt me."

"You've met it?"

"Yes, and I think I can bring Kei back. Let me try before you do this." She waved her hand toward his sword. "Kafe has called the Council." Riker had to know what that meant. All of Kei's decisions since the bite would be reversed. "They'll be here late tomorrow. Let me have the day. If Kei's not back by sunrise, you can do what you came to do."

For a moment, Riker looked like he would refuse but then she saw a glimmer of hope—the brother inside the warrior.

He nodded sharply. "You have until sunrise and then I'm coming in there."

"Thank you."

She had the chance. The dragon appeared when his mate was threatened. Now, she just had to convince a dragon that she wouldn't leave him.

She remembered the pain and betrayal she'd seen in Nekane's eyes when she'd backed away from him at the cabin. He'd seen her fear.

Mine.

The voice that had screamed that hadn't been a mature creature. Despite his size—the dragon was a child. And he didn't understand, couldn't grasp why his mate had refused him.

"I'll go with you." Riker tied his battle leathers.

"You can't. Stay here. Don't come anywhere near the cave. Nekane will sense it and it could throw off everything I'm doing. I'll be back by sunrise tomorrow."

"Lorran..."

"I have to."

"Kei's going to haunt me forever if anything happens to you," Riker warned. "Please try to stay alive."

He definitely sounded like the younger brother. "I'll do my best," Lorran said with a half smile as she began the short climb up the hill.

The entrance to the cave was shallow. The light faded within feet of the opening. In that darkness held the man she loved. And the dragon who consumed him.

She smoothed her hands down the front of her gown. She took several deep breaths. *Stay calm.* Nekane would sense her fear.

He won't hurt you. He won't hurt you.

She repeated the phrase several times before finding the courage to enter. Despite her brave words to Riker, this was still an angry and wounded dragon she was facing.

She stepped into the darkness. Light filtered in through shafts of crystal lining the far wall. After a few moments, her eyes adjusted to the low light. And she saw him.

He sat in the corner, his huge body pressed against the rough stone. His long neck was curved around, burying his head under the wing against the wall. Streaks of blood marred the green and purple scales that covered his hide—wounds he'd received while trying to get to her.

Slowly, as she walked toward him, his neck unbent and he turned his massive head in her direction. He moved laboriously, like each movement was a struggle. The glow in his eyes was dull, from pain or death, she didn't know. Or maybe it was just loneliness.

"Lorran." Her name was a mere whisper in the huge cavern. The dragon's mouth wasn't designed to speak human words. She stared into the big black eyes and a human glow flickered at her. This was Kei trying to fight free of the dragon's hold. "Get out. Go." The words were barely audible. Kei was protecting her.

But she wasn't here to talk to Kei.

"Nekane," she called. The human light disappeared and the dragon was back. She walked forward, not pausing as she walked within his reach. If what she believed was true, she needed to get Nekane to trust her, to believe her. And to do that, she had to trust him.

Those who suffered the bite of a dragon knew of only one way to defeat the beast. Common practice had always been that the human had to crush the dragon from within—to be stronger than the beast. She'd seen the dragon's power. No human could compete with that. Even Kei, with all his strength, couldn't overpower the dragon.

She had to convince Nekane he was safe.

The huge dragon head swung forward, closer, the nostrils sniffing the air. She wiggled her fingers to relax the tension that had crept into her hands.

Mine.

The sound was a mix of sorrow and resignation.

"Yes," she answered.

His head cocked to the side, like he wasn't sure if he'd heard her.

Mine, he repeated, a little louder.

"Yes," she answered again.

He moved forward, his snout stopping inches away from her. He started at her feet and moved up her body, inhaling her scent.

Male touch you?

The gravelly voice hummed with fury.

It took her a moment to remember. Riker had held her shoulders. "Yes, but he thought he was protecting me." Nekane tilted his head. "He didn't want you to hurt me."

Mine. Never hurt.

"I know."

He lowered the blunt end of his nose to her center and gently tapped against the lower edge of her stomach.
Mine.

"Yes." She would say it as many times as she needed to, until he believed her.

She was his. His mate. Standing there, with his voice in her head, and his breath on her body, she understood all that was true. She belonged to him and she had only to show him. As much as she belonged to Kei, she equally belonged to this dragon.

She slid her hand underneath the thin straps that held the gown on her shoulders and pushed it to the side. The material slid down her body, gliding across her skin and baring her to his gaze. The dragon was a sexual creature. She had to show him she didn't fear him.

Nekane ran his nose across her body.

Mine. The claim was no longer desperate. He sounded confident, pleased. Seductive.

"Yes." Her fear eased leaving only a startled desire.

Nekane's tongue slipped out of his mouth, long and thin. He traced a line along the curve of her breast. The soft fluttering touch sent a bolt of pleasure through her body. She straightened. Nekane raised his head. Naked pain blazed through the black depths of his eyes. Whether she saw it in his eyes or just felt it in her body, she didn't know, but she knew exactly what he was feeling, knew his fear. Knew he expected her to run.

"It tickled." She placed her hand on top of his nose, smoothing the soft skin between his eyes. Some of the fear eased and he began a long slow tour of her body with his tongue.

The tip of his tongue swirled across the peak of her breast. The nipple tightened almost painfully at the light abrasion. Lorran gasped. Nekane repeated the caress. His long tongue circled over her nipple, until it stood straight, straining for more. It was different from the suction of Kei's mouth but seductive just the same. She'd thought to endure the dragon's touch—to move him from this form into Kei's—but the lush press of his tongue on her skin caught her breath.

She didn't know how long he licked her skin. She only knew her moisture trickled down her legs, flowing from her pussy when he stopped. As if satisfied with the taste and shape of her breasts, he moved onward, lowering his head until his tongue touched her stomach. Then lower still. His tongue slid down her body, tasting each inch of her flesh. Then he was there, hot and damp between her legs.

Mine.

She continued her mantra. "Yes."

His tongue licked a long line up her slit, catching the juices that dripped from her soaking sex. As he trailed his tongue up, he brushed against her clit sending a spike of pleasure through her stomach.

Nekane raised his eyes.

Tasty pussy. Want more.

Lorran nodded, altruistic thoughts fading as he continued to lick her cunt. She spread her legs, opening for him. His low rumble of pleasure vibrated through her chest as he lapped her between her legs. The nimble end of his tongue swirled around her clit. Her knees weakened as the waves began to break from her center. She placed her hands on Nekane's head, using his strength to keep her upright. His tongue moved down her slit and slipped into her wet passage.

Lorran's cry bounced off the walls. It was too delicious. The long length stretched inside her, smaller but more nimble than a cock. He flicked the end of his tongue, reaching deeper, tickling her inner walls. The orgasm hit her hard and fast. Lorran heard herself yelp and her legs gave out. She plopped onto the stone floor, landing on her backside, her legs already spread wide. She stared in shock at the empty space in front of her. Nekane's tongue slid up the inside of her thigh as if collecting the moisture that had escaped from her pussy. He growled softly but she knew he wasn't threatening. It was the sound of satisfaction.

Her chest rose and fell with hard breaths as she tried to keep herself conscious. Nekane nudged her backwards with his snout. Lost in the desires of her body and the needs of the dragon, she fell back and drew her legs up, opening to him, knowing he wanted more.

Nekane rubbed his tongue along her pussy, a long slow lick that seemed to awaken every nerve in her body. Lorran gulped in air. He continued to taste her, licking her flesh. He played with her outer lips then dipped his tongue into her cunt, massaging her passage until she was begging for him to let her come.

The rumbles of the dragon's pleasure blended with her own groans.

Lorran twisted upon the stone floor, simultaneously seeking more and trying to escape the intensity. The pressure built promising completion but keeping it just out of reach. Nekane's tongue reached deep inside her sending spirals of heat through her core. She pressed her hips upward, trying to force the touch that would bring her release. He drove his tongue in shallow pulses in and out of her sex. Lorran, desperate for something to hold her to the earth, clawed at the stone beneath her as the continued caresses threw her into another climax.

Naked, spread open before him, Lorran collapsed, her arms losing all strength. He lifted his head and it was as if he smiled at her.

More.

Before she could respond, before she could think if she wanted to say no, to beg him for rest, he lowered his head and returned to licking her pussy. Lorran dropped her head onto the stone floor and gave herself over to Nekane's touch.

The only constant in her world was the unrelenting motion of Nekane's tongue, inside her sex, outside, across her skin, until her entire body shuddered at the lightest touch.

The next climax hit her, leaving her pleading. She couldn't take any more. Nekane exhaled his hot breath against her too sensitive skin and a whimper escaped.

Nekane's talented tongue circled her belly button.

"Please," she whispered. Her body was sated but the empty space in her arms reminded her of her mission. She needed to feel Kei—inside her, above her, filling her. "I need Kei."

Nekane raised his head and tilted it to the side as if trying to understand.

"I need Kei. Inside me. Please."

Kei love?

"Yes."

Love us?

"Yes," she cried, staring into his eyes. "Both of you." She realized it was true. She could love the dragon. He was a part of the man she loved. There was no way to separate the two creatures.

As if the world was made of illusion, in an instant where the huge body of a dragon had stood, there was Kei—at least physically. Nekane stared at her through the human eyes. He'd allowed Kei's body to return so he could love her, but he didn't trust enough to give up control.

He dropped to the ground, covering her naked body with his. The hard line of his cock pressed against her clit as if seeking its home. His mouth covered hers, blocking off anything resembling thought.

This was the man she loved—the man and the dragon, bound together. The dragon's power and desperation glowed in his eyes. He wanted her, wanted to love her. Just as the man had loved her body.

"Mine."

This time, the words were spoken from Kei's lips.

"Yes."

Her body was prepared and open. He slid hard into her. Lorran gasped and pressed her shoulders against the stone floor, feeling his cock deep within her.

"Mine!" Nekane and Kei shouted the word together.

"Yes."

Then they all lost the ability to speak. Need enveloped them. Each thrust inside her sent a flurry of new emotions, new sensations through her body.

She wouldn't find release soon. Nekane was finally able to fuck her, to love her with his body. She knew he wouldn't stop until he'd had his share.

He growled softly and began thrusting anew. Lorran relaxed against the ground and let Nekane glut himself on her body. The pressure grew with each plunge of his cock. Each thrust carried him harder into her body as if he wanted to become a part of her. Lorran cried out. He was so thick, so full inside her but still it wasn't enough. Her climax hovered just out of reach. She thrust up hard, driving him into her with new force.

"Nekane!" Her cry joined his growls in the open air. She held herself still and let the orgasm shimmer through her exhausted body. Long moments later, she realized the cock inside her was still. She raised her eyes and Kei stared back at her.

"Lorran."

"Kei?" She clutched his shoulders.

"I need you," he said through tightly clenched teeth. He was just barely in control. He pulled out until just the tip of his penis remained inside her and paused, looking down at the connection of their two bodies—his rock hard erection, her soft wet cunt, open for him. He moved forward and still stared, watching the long slide of his cock inside her. He pressed against her already sensitive clit and Lorran couldn't contain her gasp—a mixture of pleasure and pain.

He looked at her and the green of Kei's eyes faded, replaced by the black of Nekane. And he began to move.

She lost track of who was fucking her—Nekane or Kei. Kei would start, with the long, slow thrusts into her body. The way he'd often made love to her at the cabin, torturing her by denying her the one touch that would bring her satisfaction. Then Nekane would take over and ram hard into her cunt. Her cries became a mix of their names, her pleas alternately ignored and assuaged by her lovers. Her body was beyond her control, merely reacting without thought to the touch of the two creatures inside Kei's body.

Until all that was left was her voice crying out their names.

* * * * *

Kei stared down at an exhausted Lorran. She'd done it. Nekane was gone, sated and faded to the background. But Kei's need to reclaim his woman lingered. They had put her to hard use but he needed her. One more time, *he* needed her. Needed her eyes looking into his, needing her mouth calling *his* name.

Her eyes fluttered open. She looked up.

"Kei?"

"He's had you—now it's my turn."

The edges of her lips curled upward and she squirmed, positioning herself for the penetration of his cock. Nekane rumbled in Kei's head but the dragon stayed back, contentedly purring as Kei filled Lorran's pussy. He held her gaze until he was fully imbedded in her cunt. She reached up and brushed his long hair away from his face. He shifted his hips, resettling himself between her legs.

Her eyelids began to drift shut. He was slow, knowing she had to be sore from the hours they'd spent inside her. Still, she smiled, the contented smile of a well-loved woman.

"Hmmm, Kei." She licked her lips. "Welcome back."

"Mine," he repeated the cry of the dragon. Lorran nodded and sighed as he sank into her again.

"Yes."

It was a long slow loving, the drive only to feel each other, to be a part of each other, their climax a growing swell. The orgasm flittered through them, resonating between their bodies, vibrating until they each opened to the other. Loran moaned and felt Kei flood her again with his cum.

She was complete. Home.

* * * * *

It was over. Lorran sat astride Kei's lap, his semi-hard cock still buried inside her. She flowed over his chest, her head sagging against his shoulder. Exhaustion drained all strength from her limbs and all thought from her mind. She had no idea how much time had passed since she'd entered the cave. Hours, days, months could have elapsed.

She didn't care. She had Kei back. A vague memory of Riker's imminent return tried to insert itself but it faded into insignificance. She had Kei. Nothing else mattered.

There was no thought of moving away, of disengaging her well-loved body from his. Lorran placed a light kiss on Kei's neck. She was exhausted but she needed to feel him. His taste was familiar, an addiction from which she'd never recover. At the light touch of her mouth, his cock began to grow. She shifted, and found the energy to raise her head.

He made no attempt to make love to her, content to have her with him, to be inside her body, to lay claim to that which was fully his. He knew it. Even though the dragon was gone, for the moment, Kei the human knew he'd claimed Lorran as his. She'd never escape.

But while the dragon had taken her as his mate, Kei knew she was more. And he had to offer her the choice. Nekane grumbled. Kei ignored it.

"What's wrong?" She pushed herself up and looked into his eyes. Kei was rocked by what he saw there— loyalty, commitment, perhaps even love. But did she understand what she'd done? The dragon now assumed she belonged to them.

"Do you know what you've done by coming here?" She blinked at his harsh question. She opened her mouth to speak. Kei looked away. He shook his head and stared into the dark. Lorran's acceptance had strengthened him. He could keep Nekane at bay for a while longer. "I can feel him. He's just waiting to return. If I even think about your leaving, he crawls up inside me and—"

"I'm not going to leave you."

"If you stay with me, you'll be binding yourself to a man who'll spend his whole life fighting a dragon." Nekane snarled in protest but Kei pushed on, wanting what she offered so desperately that he knew once he accepted it, it would kill him to let her go. If she left now, there was a chance, a small chance, he might survive. Nekane growled his disagreement and threatened to take over. Kei pushed him back. Nekane could convince her to stay—Kei knew that—but somewhere in the human that lingered, Kei wanted her to stay for more than loyalty to a creature desperate for her love. And for more than sex. He wanted her love. She may be Nekane's mate, but she would be Kei's wife.

"I'll be outlawed immediately and then will come the endless line of dragon slayers. Every one of the Seven Kingdoms has laws banishing dragons and promoting their destruction."

"We'll change the laws." A dreamy smile curled her lips as if the memory was too good to hide. "And if not, we'll stay in this cave and live and make love and be at peace."

Kei didn't want to subject her to that life again. It was the life she'd had with her first husband—but there had never been peace. He didn't want that for her.

"You would go through that again?"

"To be with you, yes."

"Why?" It was the question he had to ask—even knowing he'd regret the answer.

"Because I love you."

Breath froze in his lungs, petrifying his body for a moment. She'd said it. And she had meant it. He could feel it. The instincts of the dragon gave his senses extra power.

Her heart beat at a steady pace as if the admission were no more stressful than cooking a meal.

But his human mind wouldn't accept it.

"Me or Nekane?" Kei had been there when Nekane had loved Lorran with his tongue. He'd seen her writhe on the ground, reveling in the tongue fucking the dragon had given her. Odd that he could be jealous of a creature that inhabited his body.

Lorran cocked her head to the side and smiled.

"I love both of you."

That wasn't what he wanted to hear.

"I'll never be normal. You're going to be bound to me forever."

"I already am."

He continued as if she hadn't spoken.

"I can't stand the thought of you being out of my sight. He's fighting me now. Wanting to overwhelm you. You'll never be free."

Lorran smiled. "I don't want—"

A metallic clack on the walls of the cave stopped her words.

"Lorran! Lorran! Are you all right? Are you alive? The Council has arrived."

Her head snapped up.

"We have to go," she announced.

Kei's fingers gripped her hips, not letting her move. "What?"

"The Kings' Council is here. To investigate the rumor that you've turned." She pushed herself up on her knees.

He held her in place for a moment. Lorran looked into his eyes. The black glow of Nekane's presence stared back.

"Leave?" The harsh word came out of Kei's mouth but was clearly from Nekane.

"No," she quickly reassured him. "I won't leave you, but I need Kei here to convince the others. I'll stay right here. I'll never leave you."

With her words, the darkness of Kei's eyes faded and the glitter of green returned.

It was like speaking to a child. A child in a dragon's body. With a bull in rut's sex drive. She couldn't stop her smile. She was going to have an interesting life. The thought didn't scare her as much as it probably should. Still holding his hand, unsure how much Nekane understood, she pulled Kei to standing.

"We have to—"

"Lorran?" Riker entered the cave, his sword bare and glittering. Shock and pleasure replaced the worry and tension on his face. "Kei? Hells, you've returned to yourself." He hurried across the stone floor. Kei backed away, pulling Lorran with him. He shoved Lorran behind his back and bared his teeth at his brother. Riker pulled to a stop. "Kei? What's—"

Lorran pulled her arm free from Kei's hold and slipped around to his front, placing herself between Kei and Riker. She rested her hand on Kei's chest, soothing the frightened beast inside. "It's fine, Nekane. Riker won't hurt me."

"Touch you?"

She followed Nekane's dark stare to Riker. She turned back and nodded. "Yes, he was the man who touched me but he would never hurt me."

Riker watched the exchange. "What's going on?" he demanded.

Lorran didn't look at him—she kept her attention focused on Kei.

"It's okay, Riker. Nekane just doesn't know you. He'll be fine. Won't you, Nekane?" She took a deep breath and continued to run her hands over Kei's chest. "It might help if you put your sword away." There was silence for a moment and then the slick of a blade returning to its scabbard. "See, Nekane, he's here to help." She stroked the tight muscles for a few moments more before she felt the tension begin to fade.

And Kei's eyes returned to their natural green. But he wasn't completely calm.

She could read his body. Something else was wrong. "What is it?" she asked.

Kei cocked one eyebrow up. "You're naked and my brother has now had a long view of your lovely ass."

Lorran felt her cheeks heat up. She'd gotten used to being naked around Kei. Her dress was crumpled in a pile a few feet away. She moved to get it. Kei's hand shot out and snagged her wrist. The quick tightening of his grip told her Nekane was struggling to keep her.

She smiled gently as she looked at him. "This is going to take some getting used to."

Kei stared at his hand for a moment as if he didn't recognize it. For a man who was used to ruling, being out of control was unbearable. Lorran twisted her wrist until their palms met, connecting them. She held him until he looked up. She smiled, letting him know she was fine with it. Then she led Kei over to her dress.

She turned her back to Riker, picked up her crumpled gown and released Kei's hand to pull the dress over her head. Even that distance was too much. As she raised her arms, he walked behind her and slid his hands around until they cupped the warm weight of her breasts. Her nipples were hard, long loved by Kei and Nekane. She sighed at the gentle warmth.

Lorran leaned back against him. He massaged those luscious tits that had sustained him so often and enjoyed her soft sighs.

"Riker's here," she whispered.

Damn, he'd forgotten about his brother. Now that the dragon seemed less concerned about Riker's presence, he'd turned his thoughts back to his favorite subject—fucking Lorran. Kei shook his head to clear it. As much as he supported the idea, he needed to be able to focus on other issues.

"But later, when this is all over…" Lorran turned to face him, her voice laced with promise and lust. "I'll expect you to have me, *fuck* me over and over until we're both exhausted but can't stop."

He felt his eyes widen. Lorran, using the word "fuck" so casually. He was definitely a bad influence on her. He smiled and finally pulled his hands out from underneath her gown, letting the light skirt fall and cover her.

"Trust me, I will," he promised. He took her hand again and faced his brother.

Riker's suspicious eyes were like a knife in his heart.

"Kei? Is that really you?"

"Some of the time," he answered honestly.

"What's going on?"

"It's a little difficult to explain."

"Well, start with how you defeated the dragon."

"I didn't. He's still here." Kei tapped his temple. "But he seems willing to fade away for awhile." He tightened his grip on Lorran's hand. "As long as Lorran stays nearby."

"What happens if she leaves?"

"Leave?!" The word erupted from Kei's throat but it wasn't Kei's voice.

"No, no." Lorran rushed to assure the still frightened dragon. "I'm not leaving. I won't leave you." She turned and faced Riker. "Until Kei gets a little more control, let's just keep reassuring Nekane I won't leave him. We don't need him making another appearance this soon."

"Especially not now," Riker agreed. "The Council is here."

"We'll head down the mountain."

"No, the Council is *here*. They were cresting the last ridge when I came in."

Chapter 10

"I think I'll need some clothes," Kei said, fully returning as the king. He might have a dragon living in his mind but he was still a ruler. He would continue to rule as best he knew until he wasn't able.

The clanking of bells on mules and the clomp of footsteps rang across the stone. They were here. Moments later, dressed in Riker's battle leathers, Kei took a deep breath and prepared to face the Kings' Council. As the ruler of one of the Seven Kingdoms, Kei was a member of the Council.

The Council had been created during Kei's father's reign to end the constant border wars between the kingdoms. It had been successful, with only minor skirmishes still occurring. But the strength of the Council depended on the strength of its members and if the other members of the Council decided one king wasn't strong enough, they would remove him. For the sake of his kingdom, Kei would walk out of the cave a king.

He closed his eyes and concentrated on the dragon, calling it by name for the first time.

Nekane. Nekane, I need your help. I have to go talk to —

Lorran started toward the door.

Mine leaving?!

No, she'll stay with us. Just — he didn't know what he was asking the dragon to do. Be silent and stay out of it didn't seem appropriate. *Stay calm. And quiet.* That didn't seem enough. *I'll protect Lorran,* he assured Nekane. *She'll stay nearby.*

The dragon grumbled but didn't move for control. Kei could almost see the beast pouting.

But at least it was quiet. Kei took Lorran's hand, making sure to keep her close. Nekane was quiet for the moment but Kei didn't know if he could control him if the dragon thought Lorran was in danger. The memories of those moments before Nekane had appeared in corporeal form were burned into Kei's mind. Nekane's only thought had been to save Lorran—to protect his mate.

It made the creature easier to understand.

Kei, Lorran and Riker walked out of the cave into the sunlight. A small group of gentleman, a woman, and about a dozen heavily armed guards waited. Some of the soldiers held bared swords or bows with arrows notched.

"Am I under attack?" Kei asked, filling his voice with mockery and scorn. He stared directly at his brother. The surprised look on Kafe's face when Kei stepped outside was enough to make anyone smile. Except Nekane. The crisp sharp image of Lorran being held at knifepoint entered Kei's mind. He bared his teeth and released a low growl. Lorran's fingers brushing across the back of his hand drew him back. He looked down and met her gaze. The love and support was so blatant that both he and the dragon recognized it.

Nekane backed down and Kei relaxed. He had to control this meeting. He sent a mental reminder to the grousing dragon to stay calm. Lorran wasn't going anywhere. To reinforce the thought, he pulled her in front of him.

"Brother, I believe it's still considered treason to attack the king." His voice was calm with just the right amount of arrogance. He pressed his hips against Lorran and felt her shift to accommodate his growing erection. Even with the Kings' Council before him, Kei's body was eager for Lorran's.

"You're no longer king," Kafe sneered. Desperation made his voice crack on the last word.

King Evelant stepped forward. Though there was no official leader of the Council, Evelant took charge more often than the others. "Rumor has it you were bitten by a dragon and completed the final transition."

"Well," Kei said, wrapping his arm around Lorran's waist and holding her tight against his bare chest. "I had to think of some story to tell the world while I courted my wife, didn't I?"

"Your wife?!" The lone female in the crowd shouted the question.

Kei bent forward and whispered in Lorran's ear. "Who is that?"

"My mother," she answered, barely moving her lips.

"How close are you to your parents?" he asked.

"Not very."

"That's probably good then." He straightened and called across the clearing. "Yes, m'lady, my wife. You may refer to her as Your Majesty and I graciously accept all your congratulations."

"Tell me you haven't actually married him," a small man with a rather large head announced. It had to be Lorran's father. "You are determined to make our family the subject of scorn. We'll be ruined once the world finds out you've married a dragon."

Evelant stepped forward, ignoring the interruption. It was one of the many reasons Kei liked Evelant to be in charge. He was diplomatic enough to let people talk but he stayed focused on his task. In this case, he was searching for the truth.

"We have witnesses who say you made the final transition into a dragon." He said the last word with disdain. Evelant, like others, hated and feared the beasts. He relied on warriors like Kei to get rid of them but abandoned those who sustained bites.

Nekane rumbled. Kei bent his head and placed a kiss high on Lorran's neck, behind her ear. He drew in a deep breath, inhaling her scent to keep the dragon calm.

Kei looked up and smiled. "Were those witnesses members of my brother's guard?" He scanned the rock ledge. "I don't see any sign of a dragon here." Kei stared at the six other members of the Kings' Council—almost daring them to contradict him. They looked a little less frightened and a little less confident. "Lord Kafe's been playing one of his tricks again. I go away for a honeymoon and suddenly I'm dragon-spawn."

"You're spending your honeymoon in a cave?" Evelant's disbelief was obvious but Kei was almost positive none of them had the courage to accuse him directly.

"We wanted to be alone. I thought this would be a little out of reach for most people. I was obviously wrong." He leaned down so he could look into Lorran's face. "We should have climbed higher."

She nodded in response.

"Dammit, he turned into a dragon. I saw him." Kafe waved his hand toward Riker. "*He* came here to kill him. Riker knows the truth."

Riker widened his eyes and stared between his two brothers. Then he shrugged. "Kafe, I don't know what you're talking about," Riker said. "He looks normal to me." The corner of his mouth kicked up—the epitome of the arrogant warrior. "Rather surly, but Kei's like that."

Rage radiated from Kafe's body as he turned his attention to Lorran. She steeled herself. He was obviously hoping she wasn't as accomplished a liar as Riker and Kei.

"She saw it, too," Kafe accused, pointing his finger at Lorran. "She saw him turn."

She felt Kei's fingers dig into her shoulders. She knew he was holding himself, and Nekane, in check.

She was being asked to lie. To her parents. To the Council.

To her enemy.

She tilted her head to the side in what she hoped was a look of genteel confusion.

"I don't understand what you're talking about. I've only ever seen the man that I love."

Evelant relaxed and nodded. Kafe spun around and faced him. "She's lying. They're all lying. I saw my brother turn into a dragon."

"I've never heard of anyone turning back into human form after they've made the final transition," one of the lesser kings offered.

"That's true." Lorran drew the attention back to her. "I've studied dragons for years, since my first husband was bitten. There are others who study the creatures, and no one has been able to reverse a transition." Until now, she added silently.

The small crowd milled around, clearly unsure what to do next. They'd arrived with the intent of outlawing a king and killing a dragon. What to do now that the dragon had disappeared?

"I'm sure it was all just a misunderstanding." Kei stepped away from Lorran and walked forward until he was directly in front of his twin. Lorran watched the brothers and realized they looked nothing alike. Kei had a power that came from deep inside him—a personal strength. Kafe was weak and used the power of his birth to bully others. "My brother must have gotten confused by something he saw." Kei stared hard into Kafe's eyes. "Isn't that right, brother?"

Kafe took a sharp, tight breath. And Lorran knew Nekane was staring out of Kei's eyes. Kafe swallowed and then nodded. "Yes, that's right." He turned to the Council, breaking the hold of Kei's gaze. "I apologize for any confusion."

Tension fell collectively from the members of the Council. It was obvious Kei was willing to fight for his kingdom and no one on the Council wanted to face him.

"Well, then," Evelant said. "I believe there's nothing here. We should return home and let King Kei and his bride continue with their 'honeymoon'."

"But you can't. I refuse to allow my daughter to remain married to him," her father announced to the group. "Despite what's been said, we all know the truth and I won't have my daughter married to a beast."

"He's not a beast. He's a man," Lorran countered as she stalked forward and placed herself next to Kei. She'd never talked back to her father before. She felt powerful as she stood next to Kei. "He's a wonderful king, who cares about his people and his land. He's a warrior and a gentleman. And he's the finest man I know."

Her father crossed his arms and squinted as he glared back at her. Kei had the sudden urge to protect her from her father's disapproval.

"How much will he want you when he discovers you can't bear him an heir? That's right, Your Majesty, you don't want her. She's *barren*."

Lorran tensed in Kei's arms and it was his turn to give her comfort. He rubbed his hands up her arms and eased his hard cock against her backside, silently letting her know he desired her, whether she could provide him children or not. He glanced at Riker. Riker would remain his heir and Riker could be responsible for producing the next generation.

The now familiar haze that warned of Nekane's presence was pushing at the edges of his mind. Kei smiled and had the satisfaction of watching Lorran's father lean back.

"Lorran is mine, now and forever." Kei stepped away, taking Lorran with him. He was done with this conversation. He had more important things to do. "Now, gentlemen and madam, you're on my land. My brother, Riker will escort you down the mountain and off my land." He looked at Kafe. "All of you."

Kei didn't wait to see if they complied. He turned and dragged Lorran back into the cave. Once out of the sunlight, Kei spun around and faced her.

Lorran gasped at the brightness in his eyes.

"Did you mean it?" he demanded.

"What?"

"All that you said about me to them."

The words were out there — hanging between them. She had one chance.

The dark light that glittered in Kei's eyes was a mix of he and Nekane. They both wanted, craved the answer from her.

"I love you."

"Do you? Or do you feel sorry for the dragon?"

She'd never expected Kei to be in need of reassurance.

"I don't feel sorry for Nekane. He's a beautiful creature." The memory turned her smile sensual. "With a very talented tongue. But —" she stopped Kei before he could protest. "I fell in love with the man before I ever met the dragon."

"You'll never be free," he warned, still holding himself back.

"I don't want to be *free*." She let all her love flow openly into her eyes. "I love you. Both of you. You and Nekane will learn to live together." She walked forward, finally confident in her love, in her strength. Kei needed her and she needed them. She wrapped her arms around his neck and smiled. "And until then, I'll stay close."

* * * * *

She hadn't realized how true those words would be until two weeks later.

Lorran closed her eyes and let the warmth of the sun heat her skin. She was exhausted. Kei and Nekane had been relentless, loving her, mounting her or licking her on an almost hourly basis. Today was the first moment she'd had to herself. Finally shouting that she needed a rest and she needed a moment alone, she'd locked herself in the bathing area two hours ago. More evidence that Kei and Nekane were adapting to their situation—neither had done more than playfully growl at her extended absence.

The bath was lovely—heated by hot springs and placed in a walled garden. She'd soaked in a scented tub, soothing her tired and well-loved body with the warm, spring fed water.

She reclined on the stone sleeping step and let the sun warm her body, her mind clearing from the long list of duties she had.

They'd left the cave two days after the Council had departed, when Kei was desperate for food that didn't include berries. They'd quickly found a Spirit-Guide to marry them. She might be the dragon's mate, he explained, but she would be his wife. And then they'd begun the slow process of settling into their life.

Kei had proven to all that he was in control. No man had ever succeeded in controlling a dragon. Many discounted the rumors that he'd turned at all.

Lorran was slowly learning her way around the Castle and adapting once again to royal protocol. It had been thirty years since Kei's mother had died so no one quite knew what to do with a queen. Lorran decided to make her own way and quickly set about running the Castle and assisting Kei with the daily operation of the kingdom.

It felt nice to work alongside Kei and made it convenient when Nekane or Kei decided they needed a little attention.

The boys were slowly adapting to each other. There were still battles for control. Some Kei had lost. Lorran had to calm Nekane when that happened. She smiled at the memories and let her body relax. Nekane would hold Kei back until he'd loved her long and deep with his tongue.

As she drifted into sleep, she heard the soft click of the bedchamber door opening. She sat up.

Kei was leaving?

He hadn't gone out without her. The emotions were too raw and Nekane's reactions too uncertain. The servants were just now adapting to the possibility of living with a dragon. Neither Lorran nor Kei wanted the concept turned into reality just yet.

So, where was Kei going?

Curious, Lorran stood and pulled a silk robe over her naked body. A strange voice hurried her to the door.

A female voice.

The sexuality of dragons was known across the Seven Kingdoms. That was how the myth of sacrificing virgins survived and why some women willingly went to the altar.

Lorran cracked open the door to the bathing room and felt her lip curl in disgust. This was no virgin waiting to be sacrificed. This was Mara. In learning the daily operation of the Castle, Lorran had heard much about Mara. She'd been one of Kei's favorites. She'd bragged about the hours of fucking she received from Kei. The stories still circulated through the kitchens, even now that the king had a wife.

The woman stood in the doorway, a jug of wine in her hands. And a look of pure sex in her eyes. Lorran started to interrupt but something stopped her. Maybe it was insecurity, maybe it was a wife's curiosity. Maybe it was wanting to see how far the dragon's need for sex would take Kei. The dragon lusted after Lorran. But now that he had her, he might crave others.

Lorran watched through the slight opening as Mara stepped forward and set the wine on the table.

"I was wondering when you'd call for me, Your Majesty." With a quick, practiced movement, the servant unsnapped the straps at her shoulders and the heavy gown slithered to the floor. She was naked underneath. Kei was also naked, as he often was in their chambers. Because his back was turned, Lorran couldn't see Kei's expression but he didn't look away from the servant's slim curves. It was all Lorran could do to hold herself back but she dug her fingertips into the doorframe and waited. Mara sank to her knees and ran her hands up Kei's strong thighs.

The muscles in Lorran's neck tightened to the point of snapping. Her husband stared down at the bare servant. Mara opened her mouth and leaned forward, moving ever closer to Kei's crotch.

Kei tilted his head and sniffed the air.

Lorran recognized the movement. Nekane was in charge. He looked down at the naked woman and shook his head.

"Not mine."

Mara looked up adoringly as her blond hair swished across her bare back. She blinked and smiled sweetly. "I'm sorry, Your Majesty, I don't understand."

"Not mine," Nekane repeated, a little louder than before. "Where's mine?" Nekane looked around the room, searching for his lost mate. The dragon's bellow erupted from the human mouth. Lorran ripped open the door and hurried into the room.

"I'm here. I'm here."

"Mine? Gone?"

"No, I was just taking a bath."

He pulled her hard against his body when she was within reach, completely ignoring the woman kneeling at his feet. His mouth closed over the base of Lorran's neck, licking and tasting her skin while his hands slid down her back and cupped her ass, pulling her pussy against his growing erection. Her mind blurred at the first kiss. She had just enough coherence to look over her shoulder.

"You can leave now," she told the soon to be *former* servant.

Before the door was closed, Kei had removed her robe and knelt before her, nuzzling her wet opening.

"Mine," he whispered against her skin. His tongue slipped between her folds, teasing her clit. "Mine."

"Yes," she sighed. He lifted her leg and draped it over his shoulder opening her to the deep penetration of his tongue. She gasped, the light touches against her inner walls made her pussy flow with liquid. He continued to lick and drink, filling himself with her taste. It took mere seconds for her to forget the other woman. Nekane and Kei obviously didn't remember. They wanted *her*.

Lorran held onto the bedpost behind her, leaned back and settled in for a long, sweet tongue fuck.

* * * * *

"I want her gone."

Kei's eyes drifted open. Lorran was leery of interrupting his contented doze but she wanted her position known. Kei/Nekane had fucked her for hours—

alternately licking her and fucking her until she couldn't remember her own name.

"Hmm?"

"I want her gone," Lorran repeated.

"Who?" Kei raised his head from her stomach and looked into her eyes.

"Mara? The woman who knelt naked before you ready to service you? Remember her?"

"Vaguely." He kissed her stomach just above her belly button.

"You weren't interested in her at all?" Lorran inwardly cringed as soon as the question left her mouth.

Kei lifted his head and it cocked to the side. She could tell, he was hearing from Nekane. Finally, he shook his head. "She didn't smell right." He smiled up at her. "She didn't smell like you." He drew in a deep breath and sighed. Kei stilled and then took another deep breath.

"What is it?" Lorran pushed herself onto her elbows and stared down at him.

"You're pregnant."

"What? That's impossible." Her heart thumped in her chest. Kei pulled back and stared out the open window. "Kei?" She'd never seen him like this. He blinked and then shook his head.

Finally, he turned to her.

"I think he's laughing."

"Nekane?"

"Yes. A dragon. Laughing." Kei looked up and after a moment nodded. "Something about having superior seed."

Lorran touched her stomach. A baby? She was going to have a baby? She looked at her husband. She would be able to give him an heir.

"Wait. Is it going to be half-dragon?!" she cried.

Epilogue

Twenty-two years later

Lorran stepped into the hall, her arms loaded down with packages and parcels. With this final trip, all was set for Kayla's eighteenth birthday celebration. Lorran handed her stack to Marso and sighed. They'd made it through another year without...

Screams scattered the thought even as it formed.

Another year without a crisis, she sighed, knowing that was now gone. Two young maids raced by her. Running footsteps rang across the marble floor. Several sets ran by her. One finally stopped.

"Your Majesty, you are needed."

"Yes, I'd guessed that."

Nekane's roar guided her down the hall. It had been years since he'd scared the servants. She hurried to the door of the Great Room and found her sons waiting inside, watching her husband-turned-dragon stalk a young man dressed in warrior's clothes.

Kayla stomped her foot and demanded her father stop. The dragon ignored the order and took another step toward the cringing warrior.

"What happened?" Lorran asked her oldest son, Bren.

He folded his arms across his chest and leaned against the wall. "Nekane decided to visit."

"I figured that out when I heard the screams. Now what caused it?" As she had predicted, Nekane and Kei had learned to live together. As the dragon had gotten older, his understanding grew and he no longer feared letting Lorran out of his sight. She still stayed close—for safety's sake and because the bond was as tight for her as it was for Nekane and Kei.

She turned to Rainek, her younger son. "Well?"

He shrugged. "Dad came in and found Kayla and Miek kissing. He went a little nuts."

"I knew this was going to happen," she said almost to herself as she stormed across the room.

"But, Daddy, we're in love!" Kayla tugged on Nekane's forearm. The dragon swung his massive head around. Almost-human disbelief marked his face. He glanced at the young woman and then turned back to the man pressed up against the wall.

"Well, sir," the warrior protested. "It's not really love. More like, like. Actually, we don't really know each other that well."

Lorran reached them as Kayla slammed her hands onto her hips.

"What? You said you loved me."

"Well, sure but—" He looked up at the dragon and swallowed. "But I meant it as I do my sister. I love her like I love my sister."

"You don't have a sister," Kayla sneered.

Nekane's deep throated chuckled echoed through the room. Miek slid further down the wall with each sound.

"Nekane, stop it." Lorran stepped up. She walked in front of the warrior and glared into the dragon's eyes.

"And Kei, I know you're listening. Pull him back." Kei had also learned to stay present when Nekane was in physical form.

It made for a very dangerous adversary—a dragon's body, a human's mind.

"Let him go. I think he's learned his lesson about coming near our young daughter." She turned around. "Haven't you?" Her smile was soft, but her tone was not. The young man nodded. "I think you'd better leave." Again he nodded. "And it might be best if you sought employment elsewhere." She didn't have time to watch Nekane and Kei every minute. As soon as her back was turned, they'd find Miek and begin threatening him again. It was difficult to tell what they might do, but she didn't want to find out. Though they'd been able to repeal most of the laws banishing dragons, the prejudice against dragons still existed. They didn't need to feed the fire. There was still so much work to be done.

Using her as a shield, the warrior slunk along the wall until he was near the door. He flinched when he saw Kayla's brothers waiting by the door, arms folded.

And then he was gone.

Lorran turned to her daughter. "You and I are going to have a little talk about this, young lady."

Kayla blushed but she nodded.

"Now go, all of you. And lock the door behind you."

Nekane's threats might have been fake but his anger wasn't. He prowled around the room, made tiny by his huge form.

Their three children had an equal amount of human and dragon blood. Nekane took as much pride and frustration in raising them as Kei did. It was like having three parents—and one of them could breathe fire.

When the door clicked shut, Lorran walked into Nekane's view.

"I warned you this day was coming."

Too young. She's too young, Nekane's voice slipped into her thoughts.

We'll send her to a convent, Kei mentally added, joining the conversation.

"You'll let her grow up and be a normal young woman." *Or at least as normal as a half-dragon/half-human woman could be.* Lorran kept that comment to herself. "I'll talk to her. She's just spreading her wings."

That better be all she's spreading.

"Kei..."

What did you want us to do? Let him have her?

Nekane sat on his haunches. The stubborn line of the dragon's chin told her he and Kei were in accord. She wouldn't get either on her side.

"No, but—"

Then we did right. We're done. Let's love.

One thing about Nekane, he hadn't changed his way of ending an argument. Sex still seemed to be the driving force in his life.

"I don't think—"

No. Argument done. Door closed. Let's love.

"Kei, I—"

Nekane turned his head to her and licked his tongue inside the collar of her bodice. Her body, trained from twenty-two years of his touch, melted. That nimble tongue slid inside her top and rubbed across the top of her breasts, peaking her nipples.

"We're not done with this discussion," she warned.

We are for now.

Kei's seductive chuckle entered her head along with Nekane's aroused rumble. The boys were working together. She was in for a long night.

All thoughts of protest fell away. She quickly unbuttoned her gown and stood before her love, naked and open to them. Lorran sank to the floor. Nekane pushed his broad nose against her dampening flesh. His throaty growl rumbled through his body and vibrated her pussy. Lorran gasped at the quick jolt of pleasure. His tongue licked up her legs and plunged into her sex, thick and full, almost like a cock.

Good, eh? You like my tongue in your pussy, don't you, my love? My mate?

"Yes." She couldn't stop the groan from escaping. She was open to them. The light flickered in the dragon's eyes. Kei and Nekane loving her. It had been twenty-two years but the touch of his tongue, the feel of Kei's cock never failed to excite her. She let her head fall back against the tile and let Kei/Nekane taste her. She knew from experience, she had hours before her.

My love. Kei's whispered words floated through her mind.

Mine. The word filtered through Nekane's pleased growls.

"Yes."

* * * * *

"It's not fair." Kayla plopped down on the stone steps between her brothers. "Every man I'm even slightly interested in runs away as soon as they meet Dad and if he doesn't scare them off, Nekane does." She sighed heavily and with dramatic emphasis. "I'm going to die a virgin."

Bren dropped his chin onto one hand and nodded. "I know the feeling."

Rainek followed the movement on the other side. "Me, too," he agreed.

"You?!" Kayla looked between her brothers. "You can't even begin to understand. You're *men*. I've got to wait until I'm married. Unfortunately, I'll never find anyone to marry me because of Dad. Who's going to be willing to fight a dragon for me? Because of society's restrictions *and* being the daughter of a dragon, I'll *never* have sex."

"Uh, Kayla, we're in the same boat you are."

"Only worse," groused Bren.

"How could it be worse?"

"We've got dragon blood in us," Rainek explained. "Just like you do. We're looking for our mates."

"So?" Kayla shook her head. "You can carouse to your heart's content until you've found your mates. I'm alone until I find a warrior willing to fight a dragon."

Bren sighed. "Kayla, what Rainek is trying to tell you, but making a hash of it, is—because the dragon is with us from birth, its already begun the search for our mates. We can't have sex until we find the one woman the dragon wants." Kayla shook her head, not understanding or not quite believing what she'd just heard. "We *physically* can't have sex until we find our mates," Bren clarified.

"You mean you can't...?" Bren shook his head. She looked at Rainek. "You either?"

He shook his head. "Nothing happens. It's like Dad with any woman besides Mom. No physical response."

Kayla smiled and couldn't stop the laughter that started in the back of her throat.

"Somehow I feel better knowing this."

Enjoy this excerpt from:
DRAGON'S FIRE
SHADOW OF THE DRAGON SERIES 2

The pounding inside Rainek's head and the furious ache of his arms warned him before he'd even opened his eyes that he'd placed too much confidence in Denith's ability—or perhaps willingness—to keep him out of trouble. The dim torchlight pierced his brain as he let his eyelids drift open. By all the Hells, what had happened to him?

Keeping his movements small, to limit jarring his throbbing head, he looked around. Well, it was easy to see why his shoulders hurt. Metal bands surrounded his wrists and stretched his arms up and toward the opposing walls. The bands were connected with thick chains, each link the size of a man's palm and attached to a huge bolt lodged in the stone walls. He tugged experimentally. The metal cut into his skin but he made no impact on the chain. Not that he'd expected much. When one was using chains to hold a prisoner, one didn't use soft metal.

Prisoner. The thought startled Rainek for a moment. He was someone's prisoner. But whose? And why would someone kidnap him? By the Hells, who would have the bollocks to kidnap him? His family was rich but demanding a ransom would only bring the wrath of a dragon down on their heads. Few were willing to risk that for some gold.

A faint brush of cool air drew his attention downward. He was naked, stripped of his clothes and bound to the wall at four points. A quick glance over his shoulder revealed open space behind him as well. He was situated in the center of the room, almost as if he was being put on display.

Rainek jerked again on the chains and growled when they held firm.

Patience, the dragon preached to him.

"Bite me," Rainek said without rancor and flipped his arm to wrap his hand around a link. Using all his strength, he pulled and lifted himself off the floor. Matching cuffs on his ankles stopped him from rising more than an inch. With a growl, he relaxed down.

Damn it, what good was it being part dragon if the dragon decided to sleep when they were attacked?

I can't be awake all the time. Then you *would be awake all the time.*

Rainek decided to ignore that bit of dragon logic. He didn't need the damned beast inside his head to point out the truth. They'd been ambushed and captured while they slept. Surely a dragon should have sensed that coming.

If you'd let me take my form, I might have.

Rainek closed his eyes. Denith, of course, would bring that up. During the four-day journey toward the Matriarchy lands, Rainek hadn't let Denith take his corporeal form when they'd stopped for the night. The men in his guard found it unnerving to have a dragon in their midst. Most of the guard knew that Rainek was part dragon but actually seeing that fact manifest itself was a completely different situation. Having a fifty-foot dragon share their campfire was more than most were willing to endure.

It did no good to explain that the dragon had no interest in anyone in the guard, as long as they didn't attack Rainek. Being as there were no females in his guard and the dragon viewed none of the men as potential mates, there was little chance that Denith would even notice them.

Speaking of which, what had happened to his men? He was alone in the chamber. They'd set up camp just beyond the Matriarchy boundaries. Two more days of hard riding would have brought them to the queen's stronghold.

Rainek stared at the chamber. It seemed unlikely that he'd been carried as far as the queen's castle. Despite the headache, it didn't feel like he'd been asleep for two days. The last memory he had was the tent above him disappearing and a sharp pain in his leg.

And then waking, naked and chained to the walls of a large chamber. The dim light would have allowed a normal human to see little beyond the small space in front of him but the dragon senses were sharper. Only the darkest shadows were hidden from him. Counters and tables stretched along the walls with implements and herbs he didn't want to know the use of scattered on every available surface.

Whatever this chamber was used for, it didn't look pleasant.

"I don't suppose you'd be willing to take your form now and break these chains," he asked Denith.

Denith was silent and Rainek could almost hear the beast considering the option.

Unwise, the dragon answered. *If the bands around your wrists don't break, I could end up footless when I appear. Let us wait to see who has captured us.*

Rainek yanked on the chains even though he knew the futility of it. It gave him a way to expend his frustration. He didn't care who in the Hells had captured him. He just wanted to be free.

Patience.

"Stop saying that," Rainek snarled. The only reaction was the quiet chuckle of the dragon. One of these days he was going to get his revenge on the beast.

Rainek glanced down at his chest. Along with his clothes, his amulet was gone. There was no way to contact his family. But he knew his brother. Bren was methodical and a bit dull, but he was protective of the family. If Rainek didn't check in within a few days, Bren would come after him.

The long, slow creak of a door opening shattered the irritated silence in his head. Maybe this was his answer. He took a deep breath and stood tall on his bare feet. Whoever it was, he wasn't going to be slumped over and weak when they entered.

He snapped his head toward the door, keeping his face impassive, hoping to catch his captors unaware.

He worked hard to hide the surprise as a woman strolled into the dungeon—her tall form decorated by a deep blue gown. Her breasts were small but pushed high and almost free from the tight bodice. The hint of a rosy nipple was visible. Crystalline black hair hung just to her chin, smooth and straight and with a soft swing to it as she strolled toward him. Confidence and power emanated from her.

Whispers of movement behind her distracted Rainek. He looked beyond her, curious to see who else had entered the room. He could see the bottom inches of a gray gown but the rest of the person was hidden in blackness. The first woman before him stepped forward, obviously wanting his attention.

It took his mind a moment to catch up but reality slammed into him with a sick masculine shame—he'd been captured by a woman!

The idea grated on his warrior sensibilities but logic helped him push his annoyance aside and deal with the situation.

He'd been kidnapped by the Matriarchy. Maybe the rumors were true.

Rainek felt his lips pull up in a reluctant smile. They would be disappointed when they learned the truth about him. He was the wrong man to use for a sex slave.

About the author:

Tielle (pronounced "teal") St. Clare has had life-long love of romance novels. She began reading romances in the 7th grade when she discovered Victoria Holt novels and began writing romances at the age of 16 (during Trigonometry, if the truth be told). During her senior year in high school, the class dressed up as what they would be in twenty years—Tielle dressed as a romance writer. When not writing romances, Tielle has worked in public relations and video production for the past 20 years. She moved to Alaska when she was seven years old in 1972 when her father was transferred with the military. Tielle believes romances should be hot and sexy with a great story and fun characters.

Tielle welcomes mail from readers. You can write to her c/o Ellora's Cave Publishing at 1337 Commerce Drive, Suite 13, Stow OH 44224.

Why an electronic book?

We live in the Information Age—an exciting time in the history of human civilization in which technology rules supreme and continues to progress in leaps and bounds every minute of every hour of every day. For a multitude of reasons, more and more avid literary fans are opting to purchase e-books instead of paperbacks. The question to those not yet initiated to the world of electronic reading is simply: *why?*

1. *Price.* An electronic title at Ellora's Cave Publishing runs anywhere from 40-75% less than the cover price of the <u>exact same title</u> in paperback format. Why? Cold mathematics. It is less expensive to publish an e-book than it is to publish a paperback, so the savings are passed along to the consumer.

2. *Space.* Running out of room to house your paperback books? That is one worry you will never have with electronic novels. For a low one-time cost, you can purchase a handheld computer designed specifically for e-reading purposes. Many e-readers are larger than the average handheld, giving you plenty of screen room. Better yet, hundreds of titles can be stored within your new library—a single microchip. (Please note that Ellora's Cave does not endorse any specific brands. You can check our website at www.ellorascave.com for customer recommendations we make available to new consumers.)

3. *Mobility.* Because your new library now consists of only a microchip, your entire cache of books can be taken with you wherever you go.

4. *Personal preferences are accounted for.* Are the words you are currently reading too small? Too large? Too...**ANNOYING**? Paperback books cannot be modified according to personal preferences, but e-books can.

5. *Innovation.* The way you read a book is not the only advancement the Information Age has gifted the literary community with. There is also the factor of what you can read. Ellora's Cave Publishing will be introducing a new line of interactive titles that are available in e-book format only.

6. *Instant gratification.* Is it the middle of the night and all the bookstores are closed? Are you tired of waiting days—sometimes weeks—for online and offline bookstores to ship the novels you bought? Ellora's Cave Publishing sells instantaneous downloads 24 hours a day, 7 days a week, 365 days a year. Our e-book delivery system is 100% automated, meaning your order is filled as soon as you pay for it.

Those are a few of the top reasons why electronic novels are displacing paperbacks for many an avid reader. As always, Ellora's Cave Publishing welcomes your questions and comments. We invite you to email us at service@ellorascave.com or write to us directly at: 1337 Commerce Drive, Suite 13, Stow OH 44224.

Printed in the United States
25755LVS00003B/67-408

9 781419 950377